What if she did the unthinkable?

What if she fell head over heels in love with a man whose heart would always belong to another woman?

Selena knew firsthand how badly a situation like that would turn out. But the possibility of heartbreak in the future didn't seem to matter right now.

She couldn't let Alex walk away tonight without giving him a chance to prove her wrong. So she lowered her guard and chose to ignore her apprehension.

By the time they reached her house, her heartbeat was soaring in anticipation. Just how far would they go tonight?

As far as he was willing, she decided.

Dear Reader,

I love autumn because it's a season of change. The leaves begin to fade into shades of red and gold. And the summer breeze turns crisp and cool. With the upcoming holidays on the horizon, it's a cozy time of the year.

On days and evenings like this, it's fun to light a fire in the hearth, put a pot of soup on the stove and a batch of muffins in the oven. It's also a good time to curl up with a book—or for those more tech-minded readers, an ereader.

I'm so glad you chose *The Cowboy's Family Plan* as your autumn escape. In this story, you'll return to Brighton Valley, where you'll meet rancher Alex Connor, who is determined to hire a surrogate to carry the babies he and his late wife had planned to raise together. You'll also meet Dr. Selena Ramirez, an obstetrician who has just learned that she'll never be able to get pregnant. But when a little chemistry, romance and modern science kick in, miracles can happen.

Happy reading!

Judy

THE COWBOY'S
FAMILY PLAN

JUDY DUARTE

HARLEQUIN®
entertain, enrich, inspire™
LONDON PUBLIC LIBRARY

Recycling programs
for this product may
not exist in your area.

ISBN-13: 978-0-373-65694-3

THE COWBOY'S FAMILY PLAN

Copyright © 2012 by Judy Duarte

www.Harlequin.com

Printed in U.S.A.

Books by Judy Duarte

JUDY DUARTE

always knew there was a book inside her, but since English was her least favorite subject in school, she never considered herself a writer. An avid reader who enjoys a happy ending, Judy couldn't shake the dream of creating a book of her own.

Her dream became a reality in March 2002, when Silhouette Special Edition released her first book, *Cowboy Courage*. Since then she has published more than twenty novels. Her stories have touched the hearts of readers around the world. And in July 2005 Judy won a prestigious Readers' Choice Award for *The Rich Man's Son*.

Judy makes her home near the beach in Southern California. When she's not cooped up in her writing cave, she's spending time with her somewhat enormous but delightfully close family.

To Bob and Betty Astleford,
whose family plan included me. Thank you
for all your love and support through the years. I love you!

Chapter One

As Alex Connor reached the door of the community education room at the Brighton Valley Wellness Center, a shudder of apprehension shot through him, and he froze momentarily.

Once he stepped inside, he was going to feel as out of place as a circus clown on a wild bronc, but he wasn't going to wallow in it. He owed it to Mary, his late wife, to learn all he could about surrogacy. So he shook off his uneasiness, swallowed his pride and entered the classroom, his limp a bit more pronounced than it had been when he woke up this morning.

The room wasn't full, although there were plenty of people already seated, most of them couples, whose expressions ran the gamut from hopeful to uneasy to I'd-rather-be-anywhere-but-here-tonight. And Alex knew how every one of them felt, especially the ones who looked as if it wouldn't take much for them to bolt.

A few of those in attendance were women on their own, with no husband or partner in sight. Alex did his best not to look at them, not to think about Mary, who'd had to research in vitro fertilization on her own four years ago.

Now here he was, learning what he should have learned with her back then.

Alex wasn't the only man in the room this evening, but he was the only one who'd arrived by himself. Shaking off his uneasiness, he chose a seat in the front row and placed his Stetson on the empty chair next to him. Then he waited for the class to begin.

It had been nearly three years since he'd lost Mary, along with the baby she carried. And now that he'd dealt with the grief, he was determined to do everything he could to make sure his and Mary's remaining two babies, just frozen embryos now, had a chance to live. Unfortunately, Mary had been the one who'd had any real understanding of the whole in vitro process. She'd merely showed him the papers he needed to sign and told him how much to pay, where to be and what to do. So he found himself at a bit of a loss now—and a bit guilty at not being more involved during the whole clinical part of the process.

He would have made an appointment to talk to Dr. Avery, Mary's obstetrician, if the guy hadn't retired a while back and sold his practice to a Dr. Ramirez.

Alex had planned to talk to the new doctor, but as

luck would have it, the guy was giving a series of three lectures on fertility options on Tuesday nights.

Luck, huh? Alex might have been fortunate to chance upon that flyer, but his reason for being at the wellness center in the first place had been the result of a preventable accident and an order for physical therapy.

Nearly six months ago, he'd walked behind his prize stallion, Blazing Thunder, and gotten kicked, which had been a dumb move on his part. As a result, he'd suffered a broken kneecap, which had sidelined him for months. He'd needed orthopedic surgery, and after the bones had healed, he'd been sent to physical therapy.

Last week, while working with Maria, his therapist at the wellness center, he'd spotted that poster. Because one of the topics dealt with finding and hiring a surrogate, he'd signed up to take the classes, which were being taught by none other than Dr. Ramirez.

So call it luck or fate or chance, here he was.

He'd planned to sit through this first lecture, then afterward, catch the doctor alone and pick his brain.

Mary had thought the world of Dr. Avery. Alex just hoped that Dr. Ramirez, whoever he was, would be just as competent.

So what was keeping him?

Alex glanced at his wristwatch, noting it was almost seven. The doctor ought to be here by now.

Moments later, he heard the sound of the door swinging open at the back of the room.

Footsteps clicked upon the tile floor, drawing closer.

Alex turned and glanced to the right, just as an attractive brunette wearing a white lab coat over a green dress strode toward the lectern.

Alex wasn't sure why he'd assumed that the obstetrician would be a man. It's not as though he had any qualms about a female physician; it's just that this one appeared to be too…young…too petite…too attractive.

But she certainly had an air of confidence about her.

He slowly turned to the front and waited for her to step behind the podium.

As she did so, she offered the audience a pretty yet professional smile and said, "Good evening, everyone. I'm Dr. Ramirez."

Her voice held a slight Spanish accent, although just barely, and he listened as she began covering the basic causes of infertility. Alex wasn't all that interested in that particular topic, though. And as he tried to focus on what she had to say, he couldn't seem to think about anything other than the fact that none of his doctors had ever looked like her. And was he ever grateful for that.

If the lovely Dr. Ramirez would have walked into an exam room while he'd been seated on the table, she would have had to treat him for an excessive heart rate and high blood pressure.

For that reason, he'd better rein in his thoughts and listen to what she was saying.

While he did his best to concentrate on her words, he was struck by her mannerisms: the way she cocked her head slightly to the side, the way she gripped the side of the lectern and leaned forward to make a point, the way she lifted her left hand—which wasn't wearing a ring.

Several times during the talk, he could have sworn he'd caught her looking right at him, her cheeks slightly flushed. And when she turned away to scan the audience, she cleared her throat and took a moment to skim over her notes.

Maybe public speaking made her nervous.

Or maybe she found a lone male sitting in the front row to be a little unnerving.

On the other hand, it might have been something about Alex that had caught her eye.

Nah, it couldn't be that. He'd probably just imagined her interest in him. Sleeping solo in a king-size bed for the past three years did crazy things to a man, he supposed, made him think that it was time to start looking for another woman to share his life once again.

And right now, that's the last thing Alex needed to think about. He had a surrogate to hire. Then, God willing, both remaining embryos would be implanted and he'd have two babies to raise.

As the audience broke into applause, Alex clapped, too, realizing the lecture was over and that he'd missed almost everything Dr. Ramirez said.

When she asked if there were any questions, he kept his arms crossed over his chest and let the others raise their hands instead. He had plenty of questions, of course, but most of them had to do with surrogacy, which she was supposed to discuss during the last class.

Finally, his classmates began to file out of the room, providing him with the opportunity he'd wanted—to quiz the doctor in private.

So he remained in his seat, while she gathered her notes and folded them back in the file on the podium. Then he rose and made his way to her, his Stetson in hand.

When she noticed his approach, her movements froze and her lips parted.

Her brown eyes, which were almost hazel, widened. Her thick dark lashes, natural and unenhanced by mascara, fluttered once, twice. Then she licked her bottom lip and cleared her throat.

Clearly he'd caught her off guard, so he offered her a friendly grin and said, "I wondered if I could have a few minutes of your time."

Selena Ramirez hadn't expected the handsome cowboy who'd been sitting in the front row to come up to her after her class. In fact, his presence had caused her to lose her train of thought several times during the lecture.

Who was he?

What was he doing here?

Where was his wife or partner?

And why was he coming to speak to her now?

He must have read the questions in her eyes because he added, "I'd like to pick your brain, if I may."

Goodness, right now, he could "pick" just about anything he wanted. But she shook off the inappropriate thoughts. She'd certainly provided time for questions and answers, but maybe he was too embarrassed or shy to speak in front of people. So she asked, "What did you want to know, Mr...."

"Connor. Alex. My late wife was a patient of Dr. Avery."

Selena wasn't sure what had stunned her the most, the fact that he was a widower or that he'd come to the lecture on infertility by himself.

"I'm not sure I understand," she said.

"I'd like to ask you a couple of questions that I didn't want to bring up in front of everyone else."

She could understand that, but she wasn't able to talk to him here and now. "There's a board meeting scheduled at eight, so we'll need to clear the room."

Disappointment swept across his brow, revealing an intensity she hadn't expected, an emotion she couldn't quite peg.

She glanced at her watch, a silver bangle style, then looked up at him and smiled. "But I have a little time. We can talk out in the lobby."

"Why don't we go to the cafeteria?" he asked. "I'll buy you a cup of coffee, latte or whatever."

The suggestion took her by surprise. And so did the boyish grin that set off an impish glimmer in his blue eyes.

"Please?" he asked.

She was certainly tempted. She also had a few questions she'd like to ask him. From the first moment she'd scanned the audience and spotted him sitting front and center, his hat lying on the chair next to him, she'd wondered about him. So what would it hurt to spend a few minutes with him in the cafeteria?

"All right. Coffee actually sounds good."

His smile broadened, lighting up those eyes like a Texas summer sky and knocking her completely off stride.

How was that possible? She'd never been into cowboys. Not that there was anything wrong with them. It's just that she'd always dated professional men.

Dated? Now that was a joke. When was the last time she'd had a date? Not since settling in Brighton Valley, that was for sure.

She noticed that he seemed to favor his left leg.

A new injury? she wondered. Or an old one?

Either way, she found herself heading to the cafeteria with a man who wanted to "pick her brain."

The cafeteria in the wellness center was actually a small counter area just off the lobby called The Health Nut, where they sold coffee and tea, as well as various waters, energy drinks, fruit juices and smoothies. They also provided nutritious snacks for people on the run.

While Dr. Ramirez carried her cup of coffee to one of several tables set out for those people who had more time on their hands, Alex paid with a twenty, then joined her.

"Thanks for giving me a few minutes of your time," he said as he took a seat next to hers.

"No problem."

"You're probably wondering why I signed up for your class," Alex said, his hands braced around the disposable cup.

"When I first spotted you sitting alone in the front row, I thought you might be a reporter," she said.

"I'm afraid not. I actually came to learn more about the topic you'll address during week three."

"Surrogacy?"

He nodded, then lifted his cup and took a sip. "My late wife and I had planned to have children through in vitro fertilization. We'd gotten through the fertilization process. And after the first attempt at implantation failed, we finally managed to get pregnant, but…" He paused for a moment, then glanced down at the coffee in his cup, while he relived the phone call he'd received from the sheriff's office, telling him that Mary had been involved in a car accident, that she was being rushed to the Brighton Valley Medical Center E.R., that she… might not make it.

"But…?" the doctor prodded.

Alex sucked it up, the memory, the grief, the guilt, the promise he was determined to keep. "My wife died when she was twenty weeks pregnant."

"I'm sorry." The softness in the doctor's voice, the light cadence of her accent, provided an unexpected balm to feelings that were still raw at times.

It seemed surreal now, like a bad dream. But he gave a half shrug, as if that was all there was to it, when, in truth, it was all too complicated to explain.

"So how can I help?" she asked, the sincerity in her tone, the sympathy in her eyes making him wonder if she just might hold the key to everything.

So he took a deep breath, then slowly let it out. "I

still have two embryos left, and I want to hire a surrogate to carry them. But I need to learn more about the process—the pitfalls, that sort of thing. I'll be looking for someone healthy and of sound mind. I also want to feel completely assured that whoever I choose won't have a change of heart after the implantation. You know what I mean?"

"Absolutely. Your concerns are all valid, and you're wise to learn all you can before making any decisions."

"So how do I go about finding the right surrogate?"

"What you're actually looking for is a gestational carrier because you don't need a woman to donate any of her eggs. Of course, with only two remaining embryos, you'll have only one shot at implanting them."

"If it doesn't work, I'll deal with it." He wasn't interested in going through the whole process again, unless he needed to down the line. But then again, the first go-round had been way too clinical for him to ever want to go through it again.

The doctor nodded, as if she understood.

"So where do I start?" he asked.

"You can, of course, try to find someone on your own. Oftentimes a friend or a family member will help. But there are also several reputable agencies, most of which are based in Houston, that can help you. I'd planned to give a list of them to the class during the third week, but if you'll be here next Tuesday, I can give you one then."

"That would be great." He tossed her a warm, appreciative grin, glad he'd come tonight, glad he'd asked her to have coffee with him. "I'll definitely be back next week and would like that list, so thank you."

"I'm sure you've invested a lot in the process already, but you're looking at another big investment."

Alex knew that, but he could afford it. And even if he couldn't, he hadn't touched any of the insurance money he'd received after Mary's death yet.

Still, he wanted to be sure he'd been given the right scoop. "I've heard it can cost up to a hundred grand, plus medical expenses."

"That sounds about right, although it varies with each agency. And with each carrier. Those with a proven track record will cost more." Dr. Ramirez lifted her cup and took a drink.

It was weird, Alex thought. Here he was, sitting across from a beautiful woman, having coffee as if they were friends, yet he didn't even know her first name.

He wouldn't ask—at least, not now.

"You must have loved your wife a lot," she said. "The whole surrogacy/implantation process can be daunting at times, especially when someone has to go through it alone."

To be honest, Alex hadn't been very receptive to the idea when Mary had first mentioned in vitro. He'd thought it sounded too cold, too unnatural. But rather than admit to Dr. Ramirez that he'd been less than enthusiastic at the start of the whole process, he said, "Mary was a good wife and would have made a great mother."

A shadow of emotion crossed the doctor's face—

sympathy, Alex supposed—but she didn't comment. And he was glad that she hadn't.

What was there to say? Mary would've been a wonderful mother, and Alex was sorry she'd never had the chance. All she'd ever wanted in life was to have kids and create a happy home. So when she'd learned that she wasn't able to get pregnant, she'd been devastated by the news. But she'd rallied by researching all the options available to her, and before long, she'd become obsessed with having a baby—*their* baby.

Alex had wanted to start a family, too, and had suggested they consider adoption. But Mary had refused to even think about it until they'd exhausted all their chances of having their own biological child.

He'd finally agreed, and after the second implantation had been successful, resulting in a positive pregnancy test, he'd been as excited as Mary to think that they'd finally have a little one around the house. A baby. Imagine that.

But they hadn't even had time to think about decorating and stocking a nursery when Mary had the accident.

The afternoon Alex had received the call from the sheriff's office, telling him that his wife had been critically injured and wasn't expected to live, he'd raced to the Brighton Valley Medical Center E.R., just in time to have a few last words with her. Important words.

She'd known that the baby she carried at the time wouldn't make it. But Alex still had the other embryos. And Mary had begged him to make sure they had a chance to live.

"How did your wife die?" Dr. Ramirez asked, drawing him from his somber musing.

"In a car accident."

"I'm sorry," she said again.

"Yeah." Alex cleared his throat. "Me, too."

He'd grieved Mary's death, of course, but he blamed himself for it, too. She'd asked him to pick up a list of groceries while he'd been in town, but he'd gotten so caught up talking to a couple of friends at the feed store that the errand she'd asked him to run had completely slipped his mind, and he'd gone home before a predicted summer rain hit.

Now I'll just have to go get them myself, Mary had told him.

And Alex had let her go out to her car that rainy day—a decision he'd felt sorry about the moment he'd realized how dark and ugly the sky had turned, a regret he'd have until his own dying day.

Why hadn't he made a note for himself? Why hadn't he picked up the items she'd needed before stopping to talk to Dan Walker and Ray Mendez?

Now Mary was gone, leaving him with the last two embryos to think about, to protect and nurture.

No, he told himself. *Not* embryos. *Babies. His and Mary's babies.*

But he didn't want to open old wounds any more than he already had this evening. So after he finished off the last of his coffee, he said, "Thank you for talking to me, Doctor."

"Please," she said. "Call me Selena."

Selena. It was a pretty name, and one that fit her, if you left "Doctor" out of the equation.

"All right, Selena." Her name rolled right off the tip of his tongue as if it was the easiest word in the world to say. And as he came to that realization, a smile formed from somewhere deep inside of him.

Were they becoming friends? If so, he was okay with it.

Was she?

Selena wasn't sure why she'd suggested that Mr. Connor—or rather, Alex—call her by her first name. Maybe it was because they'd somehow bonded over the time it took to drink a cup of coffee.

Or maybe they were kindred spirits because his plight was similar to her own. He couldn't have his wife's babies without the help of someone willing to carry them. And Selena couldn't have a child unless a birth mother was willing to give up a baby she couldn't keep or didn't want to raise.

Eighteen months ago, following a routine exam, Selena had learned that she'd never be able to get pregnant or carry a baby to term. The news had been heartbreaking for a woman who'd always dreamed of being a mother.

She'd hoped that with time, she would adjust to the reality and deal with it, but knowing that she'd never be able to experience the miracle of conception or go through the birth process had really begun to niggle at her lately.

Okay, she admitted. It was way more than a niggle. She'd been so dismayed, so crushed by the situation that doing her job had become more and more difficult with each passing day. Every time she thought of the miracle of conception, heard the cries of a newborn or spotted the happy tears of a new mommy holding her baby for the very first time, her disappointment grew.

At one time, she'd thought she had the perfect career. She loved delivering babies. But ever since the surgery and learning that she'd never be able to experience the miracle of childbirth herself, she'd found it getting tougher to go to the office each day.

But she shook off the melancholic thought, picked up her empty, heat-resistant paper cup and got to her feet. "Thanks for the coffee."

"You're more than welcome." Alex pushed back his seat and stood. "Thank you for agreeing to teach the class. You're providing a great service to people who are struggling with fertility issues."

She probably ought to respond and say something about being happy to offer those couples various options, but the truth was, she'd been seriously considering a career change of some kind and had almost refused to give the lecture series at all.

"Can I walk you to your car?" he asked.

For a moment, she wondered if his interest in her had been more romantic in nature than merely polite and appreciative, but she dismissed that thought as quickly as it had come to her. Alex Connor had loved his wife so much that he was determined to bring their children into the world and raise them without her.

She glanced at the handsome cowboy beside her, deciding that his offer had been a gallant gesture. "Thanks, but I'm parked in a safe place."

"All right." He lobbed another smile her way, sending her heart on a scavenger hunt for miracles that didn't exist.

"Good night, Selena."

She clung to the sound of her name on his lips, to the sincerity in those green eyes. But she cleared her voice and took a step back. "Good night, Alex."

"I'll see you next week."

Yes, she supposed he would. As she turned and strode toward the exit, she couldn't help thinking that Alex Connor was an attractive and appealing man. But she'd never dated the cowboy types—and didn't plan to in the future.

Yet even more than that, he was still devoted to his late-wife's memory. So Selena would do her best to shake any inappropriate thoughts about him.

She knew how it felt to fall for a man who'd never gotten over his first true love. And she knew just how painful a broken heart could be.

As a result, she'd vowed never to play second fiddle again.

Still, as she stepped into the parking lot, she couldn't help being a little envious of the late Mary Connor.

Chapter Two

Late Thursday afternoon, when her last patient had left and she'd closed up the office, Selena had driven to the new Brighton Valley Wellness Center.

A few days after it had opened for business, Selena had taken a tour with several of her colleagues. She'd been amazed at all the facility had to offer the community, including a rehab unit, a state-of-the-art gym, physical trainers on hand to answer questions or provide private lessons, an indoor pool, a variety of classes. But more than that, it also catered to the disabled and elderly because of its close connection to the medical center.

In fact, Selena had been so impressed with the center that she'd signed up before leaving that day, telling herself it wasn't just about becoming more physically fit. After all, she watched her diet and jogged daily. But joining the BVWC would also fit nicely into her get-out-into-the-real-world-and-start-living-again campaign.

Now all she had to do was find the time to work out, because she usually kept busy with her ever-growing practice. However, on the days she had another doctor covering for her, she slipped on a pair of shorts, a T-shirt and a pair of sneakers, just as she'd done today.

Now here she was, jogging on the treadmill and working up a sweat. With each stride she made, she pondered her options and considered the other medical specialties that had always interested her. The problem was, without going back to school and racking up more student loans, she'd have to settle on general or family medicine.

But not in Brighton Valley. In spite of the respect she'd earned in the medical community, she was giving some serious thought to selling her practice and moving back to Houston, where she'd change her specialty to one that didn't revolve around pregnancy and newborns.

That was her secret, though. That and the fact that there were way too many nights she'd found her small condominium overlooking the playground at the city park to be painfully quiet, nights when she'd cry herself to sleep.

She'd loved that complex and the two-bedroom condo. But after learning she'd never get pregnant, she'd listed it for sale. And just six months ago, after selling her first home to a couple of newlyweds, she'd moved to a quiet, older neighborhood in town.

When her time on the treadmill came to an end and

she began the cool-down process, she scanned the gym and spotted a man who looked a lot like Alex Connor. In fact, it *was* Alex, only minus his Stetson and boots. Today he wore a Texas Aggies T-shirt and a pair of sweatpants, rather than the cowboy garb he'd had on Tuesday night.

He was talking to one of the female fitness instructors—a tall, lean blonde with a healthy glow.

What was he doing here? Not that it mattered, she supposed. It's just that she'd been a little surprised when he hadn't blinked about the cost of hiring a gestational carrier to bare his children.

At the time, she'd suspected that he might own a ranch. But why was he working out at a gym in town? Wouldn't he get enough exercise from riding and roping and doing whatever else was required of him?

So who was Alex Connor?

Ever since she'd shared a cup of coffee with him, she'd found herself thinking about him, wondering about him. She'd chalked it up to her interest in the relationship he must have had with his late wife, but the man himself intrigued her.

She shut off the treadmill, then stepped onto the floor, her knees a little wobbly from the exertion. Then she started for the women's locker room, where she would shower and change into her street clothes.

Before she could get ten steps—or tear her gaze from Alex and the female trainer—he glanced across the room and noticed her. He waved, then moments later, he left the blonde's side and made his way to Selena.

"Hey, fancy meeting you here," he said.

She could say the same thing. Instead, she smiled. "It's my day off, and I thought I'd get a little exercise in."

"Do you like it here?" he asked.

"Yes, I do. It's a great facility." Her curiosity mounted until she asked, "Are you thinking about joining?"

"I would if I lived in town."

Where *did* he live? And why was he here?

She couldn't very well come out and pummel him with all of her questions, so she tossed out an easy one, hoping to get a little more information.

"So why are you dressed as if you're thinking about joining?" she asked, prodding him again.

"I'm here for a couple of other reasons, one of which is business."

At that, she couldn't help but cock a brow. And he chuckled.

"Jim Ragsdale, who's on the wellness center board of directors, wanted to meet with me today. They're interested in providing hippotherapy for adults and children with physical and emotional difficulties, and he wanted to run a couple of ideas past me."

She didn't know all that much about the program that used horseback riding as therapy for the disabled, other than those who'd taken part often showed improved balance, coordination, speech and mobility.

"It's interesting that they're thinking of adding that to their wellness program," she said.

He nodded. "I was intrigued when Jim first mentioned it, too, so I agreed to meet with him while I was in town today."

"Why the gym clothes?" she finally asked, unable to avoid a more direct approach.

"Yeah, well…" He sighed and gave a little shrug. "I messed up my knee a while back, and my orthopedic surgeon sent me to physical therapy, which I get here."

"How did you get hurt?" she asked.

"I…uh… Well, it was pretty stupid."

"Most accidents are."

Alex chuffed. "I thought I was immune to that sort of thing, but that's what I get for taking shortcuts and not keeping my mind on my work."

He still hadn't told her what he'd done, but she refrained from pushing any further. After all, his injury really wasn't any of her business.

"So what are you doing now?" he asked.

"I'm going to head home and get a bite to eat."

"Oh, yeah? Me, too. Why don't you let me buy you dinner? There's a little café a couple of blocks from here."

She wondered if he had more questions this time around—or if he just wanted to spend some quiet time with her. As appealing as the latter seemed to be, she shook off the feminine thoughts. "You don't need to buy my dinner."

"All right. Then we'll ask for separate checks."

As she pondered the invitation, shaking off the urge to agree too quickly, he added, "You probably spend way too much time around the hospital and this place anyway."

He was right. And she had made up her mind to spend a little more time getting out into the world... So she said, "Sounds good to me. Do you mind if I take a quick shower and put on my street clothes? I won't take long."

"I'll wait for you in the lobby area."

"All right."

True to her word, she returned within ten minutes. "Sorry I took so long."

"You didn't." He got to his feet, and they made their way to the entrance. He opened the door and waited for her to exit first.

How about that? The handsome cowboy was well-mannered as well. She'd have to make a note of that.

Oh, for Pete's sake. Alex Connor wasn't the kind of man she'd ever allow herself to crush on—and for several reasons, the biggest of which was the fact that he still seemed to be in love with his late-wife.

In college, Selena had fallen for a graduate student in the biotech program. They'd had something special, or so Selena had thought. She'd even started daydreaming about June weddings.

Then, when he went home for Christmas break, he met up with his first love, and their high school romance had blossomed again.

Selena, of course, had been heartbroken and had vowed never to get involved with a man who still pined over a lost lover—and that would certainly include late wives.

Of course, sharing a cup of coffee and killing an hour or so before bedtime wasn't even close to having a date or "getting involved."

"It's a nice evening for walking," Alex said, as they made their way across the parking lot and to the street.

Selena looked up at a nearly full moon and an array of bright, twinkling stars. "You're right."

When was the last time she'd taken time to gaze at the evening sky, let alone noticed the natural beauty in nature?

She couldn't remember. She'd been so caught up in her practice that she'd spent her days and nights either holed up at the medical center or at home. But she was trying to change that—first with the membership at the wellness center and maybe even with her agreement to walk to the coffee shop this evening with Alex Connor.

As they stepped onto the sidewalk and turned to the right on a side street that ran along the busier county road, she realized that Alex walked with a limp.

"Maybe we should have driven," she said.

"It's only a couple of blocks."

They continued in silence until Alex asked, "What made you want to be a doctor?"

"I don't know. I've always had an interest in medicine. And science and math were my favorite subjects when I was in high school, so it seemed like a natural career choice to make."

Her efforts had also pleased her parents, something

that was important to a girl who was the middle child in a family with seven siblings. And those same efforts had proven to be invaluable because she'd been offered a full-ride scholarship at almost every college to which she'd applied.

"Why did you choose obstetrics?" Alex asked.

Because she'd loved babies ever since the time her mother had first laid her newborn brother in her chubby little arms. But because she'd always thought her reason for choosing obstetrics wasn't all that impressive, she gave him her standard response when people asked the same question. "I found the birth process fascinating."

At least she'd found it fascinating when she'd envisioned experiencing it herself once or twice.

But enough about her. The conversation and the questions were getting way too personal for comfort, and she was ready for a change in subject.

She was tempted to start by turning his original question right back on him and ask, *What made you want to be a cowboy?*

But maybe she'd been wrong about him. Maybe there was more to Alex than a Stetson and boots.

The Aggie T-shirt he was wearing suggested he might have attended college. And he hadn't blinked about the cost of having a woman carry those embryos for him.

Maybe she'd been right. Maybe he was a rancher. After all, he'd mentioned that he lived outside of town.

Either way, if Jim Ragsdale had approached him about the hippotherapy program, his background with horses had to be pretty impressive. So he was more than the average cowboy.

Before she could ask what line of work he was in, he pointed to the red-and-white-striped awning over the entrance of the coffee shop he'd been talking about. "There it is. Katie's Country Café."

Even though the diner was located within sight of those who traveled along the nearby county road, it didn't appear to be too busy this evening.

As they neared the entry, a pregnant brunette who'd parked her weathered sedan in one of several spaces in front opened the rear passenger door and removed a preschool-age girl from her car seat. Then she waited for an older boy to climb from the car.

The mother and children walked into the diner, just in front of Selena and Alex. The boy, who was about seven or eight, spotted the refrigerator display case that held a variety of pies and cakes.

"Look," the boy said to his sister as he pointed to the goodies. "Maybe we can have dessert, Kimmie."

"Grandma will have cookies for us when we get to her house," the pregnant woman said. "So we'll just grab a quick bite to eat here."

As they all waited to be seated, a waitress serving slices of chocolate cake to an elderly couple in one of the booths in back said, "Y'all can choose any table you like."

The mother reached for her daughter's hand, then gasped and looked down at her feet, where her amniotic fluid had formed a puddle. "Uh-oh."

The little girl pointed to the wet spot and asked, "Mommy, did you potty in your pants?"

"No, sweetie. I…" The woman, her cheeks flushed, her eyes wide, glanced at Selena, her embarrassment and apprehension obvious. "My water broke."

It certainly had. And she just stood there, clearly perplexed.

"Can I call someone for you?" Selena asked, thinking the woman's husband ought to be notified.

"My mother, but that's not going to do me much good now."

"Why not?"

"Because she doesn't drive at night. The kids and I were on our way to pick her up and take her back home with us so she could help out when the baby came, but…"

"But what?" Selena prodded.

The woman paled and bit down on her bottom lip. "This wasn't supposed to happen. I'm not due for another five or six weeks."

Selena turned to Alex, who'd taken a step back and was watching the drama unfold with an expression that said he was out of his league when it came to this sort of thing.

About that time, the waitress made her way to the front of the diner with a mop. "Here, sweetie. I'll get this cleaned up for you."

The pregnant woman blew out a ragged sigh. "I don't know what to do."

"Who's your doctor?" Selena asked, reaching into her purse to pull out her cell phone.

"Martin Staley, but he's not from around here. He's in Houston. And my mom…" The woman reached for her lower belly and groaned as another pain gripped her.

Apparently, her contractions weren't going to waste any time in starting up. She was clearly going into labor—and before term.

As the pain subsided, Selena studied the woman. If the boy and girl with her were her natural-born children, she'd given birth before. So if that was the case, her labor could go more quickly than that of a first-time mother.

"Oh, no," the woman said, raking a hand through her head. "What do I do? Who do I call?"

Selena placed a hand on her back, trying to relieve her fear. "I'm a doctor, so you're not alone. How long was your last labor?"

"Two and a half hours. It went so fast, I almost didn't make it to the hospital in time. In fact, that's why Dr. Staley told me to stick close to home when I got within a month of my due date. But…" She glanced at Selena. "I thought I still had plenty of time. And because my husband left me, I'm going to need help when the baby comes. That's why I decided to get my mother tonight and take her home with us."

"Where does she live?"

"In Oakville, which is more than two hours away. I should have kept driving, but the kids were hungry. So when I saw the restaurant sign, I decided to stop and get them something to eat."

"It's a good thing you stopped when you did," Selena said. "Otherwise you would have been on the road when this happened. And Brighton Valley has a medical center a couple of miles from here."

The woman groaned and reached for her belly again. "Here comes another one. Why are they starting out so close together?"

Because this baby might come faster than her other two, which meant they couldn't very well stand here and time her contractions. Besides, there were also a lot of complications that could arise during a preterm labor and delivery, so it was best if she got medical attention as soon as possible.

Selena turned to Alex. "I'm going to have to drive her to the hospital. Would you mind coming to get me in a little while?"

Although he still appeared to be a bit stunned by all of this, he straightened and said, "No, not at all. And because the kids are hungry, why don't I order them something to go? I can bring it with me when I come to pick you up."

"That's a great idea. Thanks, Alex."

The woman reached for her purse, which had a safety pin holding one of the straps to the bag. "Here, let me get you some money."

"Don't worry about it," Alex said. "I'll get it. You'd better get to the hospital."

"If you'll give me your keys," Selena told the woman,

"I'll take you and the kids there in your car. It's only a five- or ten-minute drive."

"I hate to put you out."

"It's either that or we call an ambulance," Selena told her.

The woman reached into her purse and handed over her keys. Then she told the kids to get back in the car.

"But we're hungry," the little girl said.

"This nice man is going to bring dinner to us." The woman stroked her belly, resigned to the inevitable.

"Don't worry," Alex said. "I'll be right behind you guys."

Selena sure hoped so. One of the obstetrical residents would be the one to deliver the woman's baby. So there was no reason for her to hang out once they arrived.

But then again, someone was going to have to watch the children and figure out a way to get them to grandma's house. And she wasn't sure if Alex would be up for a task like that.

Once they were in the car and on the road, they exchanged names. "I'm Shannon Bedford, and these are my kids, Tommy and Kimberly."

"I'm Selena Ramirez. I'm going to need your mother's name and number."

"Speaking of my mom, I'd better call her. Then I'll give you her contact information."

Eight minutes and three painful contractions later, Selena drove the old Ford sedan up to the E.R. entrance and honked her horn to let the staff know she was going to need some help. Within seconds, an orderly had come out to assess the situation.

"This is Shannon Bedford," Selena told the man. "She's going to need a ride up to Obstetrics."

"Is she your patient, Dr. Ramirez?" the orderly asked.

"No, her doctor is in Houston. But she'll need to be admitted. Her water broke, and she's in active labor."

He nodded, then headed back inside for a wheelchair.

Selena placed her hand on Shannon's shoulder and gave it a comforting squeeze. "Brighton Valley Medical Center has a top-notch obstetrics ward. You'll be in great hands, so relax."

When the orderly returned with the wheelchair, Shannon took a seat as another pain gripped her.

They'd explained to the children what was happening while they'd been in the car, but little Kimberly was still worried. "Where's he going to take my mommy?"

"Upstairs to have the new baby," Selena said. "But don't worry, honey. I'll stay with you and Tommy until the baby is born. And then I'll make sure you get to your grandma's house."

Selena and the children followed Shannon through the E.R., into an elevator and on to the O.B. floor. They stopped when they reached the waiting room.

"I'm sure my friend Alex will be arriving with your dinner soon," Selena said.

They'd no more than settled into chairs near the television when Alex—thank goodness for reinforcements!—popped his head into the room. "I hope you guys like grilled cheese sandwiches and chicken tenders."

"We do," Tommy said, getting up from his chair. "Thanks."

"I also brought milk to drink and cookies for dessert," Alex added, as he placed the bags on a nearby coffee table.

Selena couldn't help but grin. The cowboy was proving to be both thoughtful and generous.

After setting out the food and watching the children take seats on the floor around the coffee table, Alex nodded for Selena to step off to the side. As she did so, he lowered his voice. "How's their mother doing?"

"She's already been admitted and is being examined now."

"Is everything going to be okay?"

"I called her doctor in Houston and let him know what was happening. He said the baby was breech at her last appointment. Unless it's turned, the delivery will be more complicated. She's also nearly six weeks early, but Dr. Chin, the resident in charge, is competent. So I'm sure everything will be okay."

"What about the kids?" he asked. "What are you going to do with them?"

"I'll wait here until Shannon is out of delivery. Then I'll drive them to Oakville to stay with their grandmother."

"Are you taking her car?"

"No, it was making some weird noises on the way here, so I'd rather take my own. I'll have to transfer the car seat, though." The minutes the words were out of her mouth, she realized she'd have to ask Alex to give her a ride back to the wellness center.

"Okay," he said. "I'll just hang out here until you're ready to go back."

"You don't have to do that."

"I know." His gaze locked on hers, and for a moment, she felt as though they were a team.

Selena couldn't remember the last time she'd felt like she had someone on her side—a friend, a lover...

Oh, for Pete's sake. They might be developing a friendship, but they'd never become lovers.

Before she could tear her gaze from his and get her mind back on track, Ella Wilkins poked her head into the doorway. "Dr. Ramirez?"

Selena's gaze moved from the handsome cowboy who was proving to have a protective streak to the obstetrics nurse who'd just arrived. "Yes, Ella?"

"Dr. Chin has decided on a C-section and wanted to know if you'd assist."

Selena stiffened. "Of course. I'll be right there."

"He's also put out a call for Dr. Parnell," Ella added.

Roger Parnell was a neonatologist, who'd be in charge of the baby when it was born. It was standard procedure in a C-section, but had something unexpected happened?

Why was Darren Chin asking her to assist?

Selena turned to Alex, who was no longer smiling.

"What can I do to help?" he asked.

"Watch the kids. I'll be back as soon as I can."

She just hoped she wouldn't have to bear bad news to Shannon's children when she returned.

Chapter Three

Alex didn't have any idea what was going on beyond the double doors that led to the obstetrics unit, but he was glad Selena was in there with the kids' mother.

He'd always been uneasy in hospital settings, and even more so after Mary's accident. In fact, when he'd entered the main lobby of the medical center tonight, carrying the takeout food, his gut had clenched and his steps had slowed. The memory of that rainy afternoon he'd rushed to the E.R. to be with his dying wife had slammed into him, knocking him off stride.

He'd shaken it off the best he could, telling himself he had a job to do, kids to feed. So he'd bypassed the hospital volunteers who guarded the lobby entrance and went right for the elevator. All the while, his heart had pounded like a son of a gun, but he'd pressed on.

Selena had told him she'd be in the waiting room just outside the maternity ward. And that's right where he'd found her.

Once he'd entered the small room and seen Selena and the children seated together and watching some animal show on television, his pulse rate had slowed to a normal pace and the painful memory had faded away.

Selena had looked up and blessed him with a smile that had gone a long way in chasing off the bad memories and promising to create a new one. But before either of them could speak or move, a nurse in scrubs entered the room.

As soon as Alex heard her say "C-section" and watched Selena's expression turn somber, all those dark memories he'd held at bay came flooding back.

Most people came to hospitals to get well, to heal. But some, like Mary, weren't that lucky. And Alex couldn't seem to shake the feeling that things weren't going as expected in delivery.

Thank God Selena was in there now.

It was weird, though. He had no personal knowledge of Selena's medical skill, yet just knowing she was with the pregnant mother provided him with an inexplicable sense of relief. For some reason, he was convinced the mother and her newborn were in good hands.

When it came time for his babies to be born, he hoped the doctor delivering them was a lot like Selena.

Alex glanced at the clock on the wall. How long did this sort of thing take? When would Selena come back?

He wasn't sure how he'd gotten involved in all of this

in the first place. He'd just been at the wrong place at the wrong time, he supposed.

Either way, he'd do his part by looking after the pregnant woman's children. Only trouble was, he didn't have a clue what to do with them, other than to feed them and let them watch television. So he'd just have to wing it.

At least they seemed to be good kids—quiet, obedient. But what did he know? They were probably scared, just like he was.

For a guy who was determined to be a father, he sure didn't know much about raising children. Was he going to have to take some parenting classes, too?

Probably, although he had no idea where something like that would be offered. He'd have to ask Selena about it.

Again he looked at the clock. What was keeping her?

"Hey, look, Kimmie." The boy pointed to the television screen, where a commercial for kitty litter filled the screen. "Doesn't that cat look a lot like Whiskers?"

The girl looked up and nodded. "Only Whiskers has more white on his paws."

Alex made his way to the oak coffee table, where he'd spread out the grilled cheese sandwich and the chicken fingers he'd purchased at the café. He spotted the bag that still held the coffee he'd brought back for him and Selena to drink.

Would she still want it? It would probably be cold by the time she returned.

He'd sure feel a lot better if she were here with him

now. He reached into the sack, removed one of the heat-resistant cups and took a seat near the children.

So far, so good, he thought. But they'd be finished eating soon. Then what was he going to do with them?

God only knew. In the meantime he tried to focus on the television screen, rather than the slow-moving clock on the wall.

Hopefully, Selena would be back before word got out that he was completely out of his element when it came to dealing with kids.

At 9:47 that evening, Michael Allan Bedford entered the world, red-faced and squalling. Even at four pounds two ounces, the little guy seemed to be a fighter, which was a good sign that he'd have little trouble while in the new neonatal intensive care unit.

Selena had assisted the delivery which had been fairly uneventful, then she'd followed Shannon's gurney into the recovery room, where she took note of the grandmother's name, address and phone number.

"As soon as you're taken to your room, you can give your mom a call," she told Shannon. "But in the meantime, I'll let her know that everything is okay—and that I'll be taking the kids to her within the next hour or so."

"I don't know how to thank you for all you've done for me, for all you're doing." Shannon's eyes filled with tears.

"I'm glad I was there when you needed me," Selena said.

"Me, too. You've been a real godsend, Dr. Ramirez."

Selena had just done what most women or doctors would have done in her place. But she thanked Shannon just the same and said, "I'll stop by to check on you tomorrow."

Then she went to find Alex and the kids.

When she reached the doorway to the waiting room, she spotted little Kimberly stretched out on the small love seat in the corner, sound asleep. Tommy and Alex were sitting on the floor in front of the coffee table, a coloring book and crayons spread out before them.

So Alex truly *was* daddy material. A smile stretched across her face, and she remained in the doorway for a moment longer, taking it all in.

As if sensing her presence, Alex glanced up. His gaze immediately sought hers, seeking an answer to the question he hadn't needed to ask.

She nodded and offered him a weary smile, letting him know that the mother and baby were both doing fine.

"Hey, Tommy," Selena said, as she made her way into the room. "Your mom wanted me to tell you that your baby brother has been born."

"Cool." The boy scrambled to his feet and hurried to Selena. "Can I see them?"

"Not yet. Your mom will be in recovery for another hour or so, and the doctors are still examining the baby. But he looks good. They both do."

If all went well, the pediatrician might even release little Michael within the next week, although the jury was still out on that.

She wondered if it would be difficult for Shannon to leave her newborn in the hospital of a strange town and go to her mother's house, which was more than an hour away. Probably. Most new mothers wanted to keep their babies close. But there wasn't anything Selena could do about that. Right now, she had a promise to keep—to see that the children were delivered to their grandmother.

"I'm going to need that ride back to my car at the wellness center," Selena told Alex. "I have to drive the kids to Oakville."

"Do you have an address?" he asked.

"Yes, I do."

"Good. We can take my car. I'll drop you off at the wellness center when we get back."

"You want to go with me?"

He flashed a smile at her that lit up every raw spot in her heart, exposing every pain and disappointment she'd ever had—at least, in her own mind.

Torn between the wisdom of traveling with him and the desire to have him come along for the ride, she asked, "Are you sure? You didn't sign on for all of this."

"Neither did you. Besides, it's getting late. There's no reason for you to go all that way alone." His gaze sought hers, creating a connection she could almost feel, she could almost…trust.

She pondered his offer, but only for a moment. Why insist that she could handle the drive on her own when she had someone willing to go with her? And not just anyone, but a handsome cowboy who threatened to turn her heart every which way but loose.

"Okay," she said. "I'll take you up on that."

"Good."

Was it? She certainly hoped so.

"Tommy," Alex said, "if you'll put those crayons and coloring books back where we found them, I'll pick up your sister and carry her to my truck."

"Will we all fit?" Selena asked.

"It's a dual-wheel Dodge with a king cab. So we'll be fine, although we'll need to transfer that car seat."

As Alex tenderly scooped a sleeping Kimberly up in his arms, triggering visions of home and heart and family, he said, "Let's not keep Grandma waiting."

For the briefest of moments, Selena wondered what it would be like to have a family, but she brushed off the thought as quickly as it had sparked.

The cowboy had a family plan already in place, and it didn't include her.

In spite of the late hour and a minimal amount of cars on the road, the drive to Oakville took nearly two hours, so Alex and Selena would be pulling an all-nighter before getting back to Brighton Valley. But Alex didn't mind. He liked having the pretty doctor ride shotgun with him, sharing her company as well as a smile or two.

On the way to Oakville they hadn't done much talking. When they did speak, they kept their voices down so they wouldn't risk waking the children who slept in the backseat.

Once they'd reached the small tract home on Blue Ridge Court, Ruth Morgan had welcomed them inside and showed them to the spare bedroom, where the coverlets on two twin beds had already been turned down, awaiting her grandchildren.

After Alex had carried the kids from the car and they'd been tucked in, Ruth had thanked them again for making sure her daughter got to the hospital and for bringing the kids all the way to Oakville.

"I would have jumped in the car and met you in Brighton Valley," she said, "but I'm having some vision problems, and the doctor won't allow me to drive at night."

"I'm glad we were there when Shannon needed us," Selena said. "Maybe after you talk to her in the morning, the two of you can figure out a way to pick up her car. She'll also need a ride home from the hospital in a couple of days. In fact, because she had surgery, she won't be allowed to drive either—at least for a few weeks."

"I'll call my church first thing in the morning," Ruth said. "I'm sure I'll find someone who can help out."

Alex was glad to know the woman had options. And because it appeared their job was through, he said, "We'd better hit the road."

"All right," Ruth said. "But wait here for a moment. I fixed you a snack to take with you—oatmeal cookies. And I prepared a thermos of coffee. It'll help keep you awake on the way home."

She'd been right. The caffeine and sweets had helped. So had a late-night radio station that played classic country music.

By the time Alex spotted a sign that claimed Brighton Valley was twenty miles away, the sun had begun to rise, painting streaks of orange and purple in the east Texas sky.

"Do you have to work today?" Selena asked.

"There's always work to be done on a ranch, but I might find time for a nap. We'll see." Alex shot a glance across the seat at his lovely passenger. "How about you?"

"I have patients coming in from nine to five, so a nap's out of the question. But at least I'm not on call today. One of my associates is going to have hospital duty, so I can turn in early this evening and catch up on my sleep."

It was becoming clear to Alex that Selena was a good doctor—and that she had a great bedside manner.

For a moment, his sleep-deprived mind veered far away from hospital beds and gowns and medicinal smells. Instead, he wondered just what kind of bedside attention a man like him might get from a woman like her, what kind of silky sleepwear she might choose, what kind of tempting perfume. But he shook off the inappropriate thoughts and scolded himself for getting so far off base.

"Mary used to think the world of Dr. Avery," Alex

said. "So I was a little disappointed to learn that he'd retired. I didn't know him very well, but I'd hoped his replacement was just as good."

Selena turned to him, her expression suggesting that she was waiting for his assessment of her.

He tossed her a smile. "I was impressed with you tonight, Selena. You're going to make a fine replacement for Doc Avery."

A slow smile stretched across her face, lighting her eyes. "Thank you."

He returned his gaze to the road, although he wished he could keep his mind on track just as easily. But it was hard to do when he couldn't help thinking that Selena was an amazing woman. She'd stepped right in to help a laboring woman who wasn't her patient, when she could have called in paramedics. Then she'd stuck around after the surgery and had lost a night's sleep to see that Tommy and Kimmie were delivered safely to their grandmother's house.

As something warm and tingly spread through the cab of his truck, he reached for a safe topic to tackle. One that wouldn't have him tripping all over himself to sing her praises.

"Where did you go to college?" he asked.

"Baylor University. How about you?" She pointed at the shirt he wore. "Is it safe to assume you're a Texas A&M alum?"

"Yes, I am."

"So the cowboy hat, jeans and boots you were wearing last Tuesday night was just a prop?" she asked.

"Not at all. I'm a cowboy through and through."

"Oh, yeah?"

His dad, if he'd still been alive, would have had the same reaction. But then again, his uncle had been more an of influence on Alex.

"So you grew up on a ranch?" she asked.

"Actually, I spent the first ten years of my life in Dallas. I never even rode a horse until after I moved to Brighton Valley."

"How did you end up there?"

"When my dad died unexpectedly of a heart attack, my mom sold the house in the city and moved in with her brother. She'd been raised in the country and wanted me to have the same experience."

"So the city kid morphed into a rancher?"

"That's pretty much how it happened. It didn't take long either. My mother always said I'd been born with a cowboy's heart. And she's probably right. I can't imagine what my life would have been like had I remained in Dallas. It seems as if I was meant to be a rancher."

In fact, he hadn't even wanted to leave the Rocking B to attend college, but the details of his father's trust had not only provided for an education, but had pretty much locked him into one, whether he wanted one or not. So while his dad—if he'd still been alive—might have insisted he attend law school or get an MBA, Alex had chosen to go to Texas A&M, where he got a degree in animal science, something practical he could use back on his uncle's ranch.

They continued to drive in silence, and he wondered

if they were both thinking the same thing. How had such a chance meeting turned into…well, whatever this was? A friendship, he supposed.

But just being with Selena this evening made him realize that he'd been living on the periphery of life ever since Mary's death. And that maybe it was time to cross over to the real world again.

When they reached the turnoff to the wellness center, the sun had begun its slow rise. Alex followed the driveway into the parking lot, where Selena's white Lexus was the only one left.

He pulled into the space next to hers, then shut off the ignition. It wasn't necessary, he supposed, but he got out of the car anyway. He told himself it was to make sure that she got into her vehicle okay, that it started right up. That she wasn't stranded in a parking lot while he was driving off to his ranch.

Who was he kidding? He wasn't quite ready to say goodbye. At least, not from inside his truck.

"I see you're chivalrous, too," she said.

"Too?" Had she been keeping a list of his qualities?

She flushed, then glanced down. "I'm sorry. Just a little slip of the tongue."

He knew she was talking about her choice of words, yet the thought of tongues slipping set his imagination soaring.

There he went again, veering dangerously off course.

"I guess the lack of sleep makes you say and think all kinds of things," he said.

"You've got that right." She reached into her purse,

then pulled out a set of keys. "Oops. These are Shannon's. I should have left them with Ruth."

"Since her car is still parked in front of the hospital, we probably ought to give them to Shane Hollister," Alex said.

"The sheriff?"

"Wouldn't you hate to see Shannon get a parking ticket?"

Selena nodded. "Poor thing. She's really got her hands full. That's the last thing in the world she needs right now."

Alex didn't respond.

He didn't move either. He just stood there, watching as Selena fumbled around in her purse again.

After a moment, she broke into a beautiful smile and removed her hand, dangling another set of keys. "Good news. I found mine."

For the life of him, he couldn't manage to agree. That it was good that she'd found her keys. That it was time to say goodbye.

How could he? He wasn't quite ready to see her drive away and end a most unusual—and surreal—day.

So how in blazes did he go about prolonging it when they were both tired, when they both needed to go home and get ready to face a new day?

In spite of his better judgment, in spite of the fact that sleep deprivation led to accidents, he placed his hand on her cheek. "It was an interesting evening—and so much better than watching TV. I'm glad I spent it with you."

Then he did something he'd probably live to regret—
or, after getting some shuteye, he'd *wake* to regret.

He lowered his mouth, intending to brush a kiss on
her cheek, yet finding her lips instead.

The last thing in the world Selena had expected from
Alex had been a goodnight kiss, but she'd been too surprised by the move to stop it.

As his mouth met hers and she caught his musky
scent, she held not only her breath, but every thought
and whisper and dream she'd ever had.

Who was this man?

And what was he doing to her?

As the kiss deepened, as their lips parted and tongues
touched, she thought she might swoon. So she gripped
the fabric of his T-shirt and held on for dear life.

The kiss was amazing. What began soft and sweet
evolved into the kind that could make a woman lose
her head. Her mind spun out of control as she tried to
make sense of it all—the allure of his kiss and the effect it had on her—but it was over before she knew it,
leaving her stunned and speechless.

And yearning for more.

Alex straightened and blessed her with a boyish grin.
"I meant to aim for your cheek."

"You missed."

"Yeah." His grin deepened to a full-on smile. "Sorry
about that."

Was he? Because she darn sure wasn't.

And shouldn't she be?

"Drive carefully," he said.

Yeah. Right. Her cue to leave and to segue from the awkward to the familiar. She needed to get into her car and drive away. Yet something held her here. Lack of sleep, she suspected. And maybe the easy camaraderie they'd shared on the trip back from Oakville. Yet there was something else going on, too.

Selena hadn't been that unbalanced by a kiss in a long, long time—if ever. But she did her best to steady herself, to get back on track and pretend that they'd reached that level of friendship where an affectionate parting was the norm.

Eager to escape the confusion, she reached for the door handle, using the keyless entry, and slid behind the wheel. "Thanks for riding with me and helping with the kids."

"My pleasure."

"Have a good day," she said as she reached to pull her door shut.

"You, too."

She didn't know about that. Her day was already off to a surreal start. How was she going to keep her mind on her work and on her patients when she'd be reliving that kiss for the rest of her waking hours?

Then there'd be those bedtime hours, when it was sure to come back and haunt her dreams.

After shutting the car door, she pressed the button to start the engine. Then she slowly backed out of the parking space, trying to put a little distance between her and the man who'd set her off course.

Once she reached the exit and prepared to pull out on to the street, she glanced in the rearview mirror and spotted Alex still standing by his truck.

But she feared that neither of them was in the same place they'd been before they'd started out last night.

That unexpected kiss had linked them in a way she hadn't anticipated and set off a slew of romantic thoughts and yearnings, which was too bad.

The last thing in the world she needed to do was to imagine herself playing house with a handsome cowboy who was still in love with his late wife.

Chapter Four

After leaving the wellness center, Selena arrived at her new two-bedroom digs on Hawthorne Lane, one of the older neighborhoods in Brighton Valley. She checked her voice mail, took a quick shower and dressed for the day. While tempted to grab something she could eat on the run, she took time for a good breakfast—a veggie omelet, a fruit cup and a blueberry muffin—to fuel her body and keep her going until noon.

It was almost seven-thirty when she made the fifteen-minute drive to the medical center, which was just a few blocks down the street from her office.

Because she still had an hour before her first patient would arrive, she decided to swing by the hospital so she could check on Shannon and her baby.

Her first stop was at the neonatal intensive care

unit, where little Michael slept in a heated isolette. He wasn't the tiniest baby in the NICU, but at just over four pounds, he was still smaller than a full-term newborn.

Last night, while Shannon had been in labor, his heart rate had dropped, indicating he was in distress, so Dr. Chin had decided upon an immediate C-section. His initial Apgar score had been a little low, but Roger Parnell, the neonatologist at the delivery, hadn't been too concerned. And thank goodness Michael's subsequent scores had improved.

His color looked good today, Selena decided, as she studied the sleeping newborn. Her medical assessment soon took a maternal shift, and she found herself taking note of his little fingers and toes. He was a beautiful baby, with dark tufts of hair…. And look at that sweet little grimace on his face.

"Good morning, Dr. Ramirez."

Tearing her gaze from the newborn, Selena turned to Margie Kaufman, the charge nurse, and offered her a smile. "Good morning, Margie. I stopped by to check on Baby Bedford before visiting his mother. How's he doing?"

"So far, so good. He doesn't seem to have any major issues, although we're watching him closely. We'll probably bring his mom in to visit later this morning."

"I'll let her know. I'm sure she's eager to see him." Still, Selena made no immediate move to leave. Instead, she continued to watch little Michael and to imagine having a baby like him someday. But longing for something that wasn't meant to be wasn't doing her any good, so she forced herself to leave the NICU and head for the maternity floor. When she reached the nurses' station, she learned that Shannon Bedford was in room 407.

Moments later, she found her sitting up in bed, her breakfast tray in front of her.

"Good morning," Selena said. "How are you feeling?"

"Sore, but I guess that's to be expected."

"I'm afraid so. Dr. Chin should have ordered pain meds for you."

"He did. I had a shot a few minutes ago. Well, an injection into my IV. I hate it, though, because it makes me feel loopy and weird." Shannon pushed her half-eaten tray aside. "How are the kids?"

"They're fine."

"Did you have any trouble finding my mother's house?"

"No, not at all. The drive was easy. Alex, my... friend, went with me to Oakville."

"I don't know how to thank you. Would you please let Alex know how grateful I am? He's a darn good friend in my book."

Selena suspected that Shannon was right, although she was still trying to wrap her mind around the whole "friend" idea.

Somehow, as the evening wore on, they'd become more than acquaintances, that's for sure. And that good-night kiss had her wondering if they'd become even more than friends, at least in his eyes. But rather than ponder that possibility, she decided to chalk the whole thing up to exhaustion and relief that the ordeal was over.

"Where did you meet him?" Shannon asked.

The question struck Selena as being unusual, but the events that had unfolded last night had all been a little dreamlike. And she found herself saying, "At the wellness center down the street. He took a class I offered."

No need to mention anything about the topic of the class. Or the fact that Alex was determined to find a woman to carry his and his late wife's unborn children. But maybe Selena would be wise to make a note of that, to keep in mind that Alex and his wife must have had a good and loving marriage.

Would Selena ever find a man who cared that deeply for her, even if she died?

"Are you dating him?" Shannon asked. "Not that it's any of my business, of course. It's just that... Well, I don't know why I even asked. I'm sorry. I've always been a little too nosy for my own good. And a little impulsive." She blew out a ragged breath and clucked her tongue. "Just look where that impulsiveness landed me."

Now it was Selena's turn to be nosy. "I'm not sure I'm following you."

"I met this guy—Joey Delgado—in a bar one night. I'm a little embarrassed to admit this but I went home with him. We dated a week or so, then called it quits. He was about five years younger than I was. And I had kids. I should have known something solid wouldn't have worked out."

Selena met her first love, a graduate student, in college. And that hadn't worked out so well either. Sometimes the whole dating thing was a complete crapshoot, if you asked her.

"Do you plan to tell him about the baby?" Selena asked.

"I don't know."

Silence stretched between them for a moment. Then Selena said, "I stopped by the NICU earlier."

"How's the baby doing?" Shannon asked.

The fact that she'd asked about Michael as a second thought struck Selena as a little unusual. Most mothers in her situation would have been more...

No, it was wrong to make those kinds of assumptions. After all, Shannon probably had a lot of other things on her mind, like two children who'd been transported by strangers to stay with her mother, bills to pay, a new day care dilemma and probably a lot more than that. Besides, she'd just been given an injection for pain, which she claimed made her feel "loopy."

"I thought being a single mom with two kids was tough," Shannon added. "But now look at me. I'm still single and have three."

Selena wondered if Shannon would consider adoption as a solution to her problems. At that rogue thought, a seed of hope surged through her, but she didn't dare let it take root and blossom.

After all, when someone finally wheeled Shannon to the NICU to see that precious little boy for the very first time, she was going to bond with him. And where would that leave Selena and her dream of instant motherhood?

Disappointed yet again.

So she put it all behind her—Shannon and her newborn, Alex and the unexpected kiss—then went back to the office to focus on her practice and her patients.

And it worked beautifully—until Tuesday night, when Selena arrived to teach the second class.

Once again, she found Alex sitting front and center, his Stetson resting on the chair next to him.

She hadn't seen him for five days, since the night Shannon's baby was born. Of course, there'd been a good reason for that. She'd avoided going to the wellness center, hoping she wouldn't run across him there. Instead, she'd exercised at home and jogged in the neighborhood.

But now here she was, trying to focus on her notes and her presentation, which was even more difficult to do this evening than it had been last week before they'd spent time together.

And before he'd kissed her.

She tried her best to pretend it had never happened and that he wasn't back in full force—a cowboy to be reckoned with. So while she did cast an occasional glance his way during her lecture, she kept her focus on the others in the room, on their questions.

And just like he'd done last week, he'd waited until the room had begun to clear before walking up to the podium.

"Hey," he said, flashing a heart-thumping grin her way. "Did you catch up on your sleep the other day?"

"Eventually." She returned his smile with one of her own. "How about you?"

"I didn't get a nap like I'd planned, so I made it an early night." As she gathered her notes, she paused, her lips parting. "Oh, I nearly forgot. I brought that list of agencies for you." She reached for a sheet of paper at the back of her stack and handed it to him.

"Thank you." He glanced at it for a moment, then rolled it up and placed it in his hip pocket.

She supposed he had no place else to put it, but he seemed to discard it without much fanfare. Was that a sign that his plan to have his wife's children was fading?

As she closed her file of notes, she caught a hint of his musky scent and, when added to the rather intoxicating sound of a slight southern drawl, the whole effect was entirely too sexy to ignore.

"Have you eaten dinner yet?" he asked.

Her movements froze. Was he asking her out?

Oh, for Pete's sake. Joining him for a bite to eat wouldn't be a date. If he'd had a romantic interest in her, he would have said or done something on the night they'd driven the kids to Oakville.

Okay, so he'd kissed her at sunrise, which had been surprisingly sweet and romantic. But that could have been his way to end their unexpected nocturnal adventure. Right?

So she said, "No, I haven't eaten yet. But I have some leftover chicken vegetable soup I'm going to warm up when I get home."

As he took a step closer, that arousing cowboy scent,

all musky and manly, played havoc with her senses, making her wonder just what he was really thinking.

"Why don't you save that for lunch tomorrow," he said. "I'd like to take you to Emilio's tonight. I've been craving some Italian food, and that's the best place in town to get it."

His suggestion was tempting—and for a lot more reasons than an empty stomach. Yet instead of coming up with a polite way to decline, she said, "Okay. Why not?"

"Good. I hate eating alone."

All right, then. He'd only suggested they dine together as a friendly offer. She was relieved to know she'd been right about his motive.

Yet being right was a little unsettling, too—and maybe even disappointing. So why was that?

Probably because if things were different, if they'd met elsewhere, if he wasn't determined to see his late-wife live on by having the family they'd once planned…

Enough of that. The compulsion to analyze everything was going to drive her crazy, so she slipped her notes into her purse, determined to let it all go. But when she glanced up and spotted a glimmer in his eyes, her heart skittered to a stop, and she found herself trying to read into his expression, his smile.

Maybe going out to dinner with him wasn't such a good idea, after all.

Still, she followed the handsome and mesmerizing cowboy out of the wellness center and to his truck.

As she walked beside him, she couldn't help noting that he seemed to have lost his limp in favor of a sexy swagger. A girl could really lose her head around a man like him. She just hoped that wouldn't be her fate.

Alex had no idea why he'd suggested they eat at Emilio's, one of the newest restaurants in town—and one of the more romantic. He'd told Selena that he liked Italian food, which was true. But there'd been better, more casual places he could have suggested, like Pistol Pete's Pizzeria and Mama Mia's Italian Kitchen, both of which were located in nearby Wexler and not that far away.

Instead, here they were, sitting across from each other at a white linen-draped table for two, which had been adorned with a candle and a single red rose in a bud vase. As they sipped glasses of Chianti, a crooner in the adjacent lounge sang "That's *Amore*."

A dinner didn't get much more romantic than that, Alex supposed. Not that he minded. He was a bit too dazzled by the lovely woman sitting across from him.

Selena Ramirez might be a respected doctor, but right now, with the candlelight providing a warm and cozy glow, the wine offering just enough of a buzz to lower one's guard, she was everything a man might want in a woman: petite and shapely, with soulful brown eyes the color of fine Tennessee bourbon and lush dark hair that cascaded over her shoulders.

Of course, he'd best keep reminding himself that she was merely a dinner companion and not a date. But the longer they sat here, the more difficult it was to keep things casual between them.

Just moments ago, the waiter had taken their dinner order, leaving them to chat. Alex had done his best not to ask everything there was to know about her, thinking it would be pushy and out of line if he did. But that didn't quash his mounting curiosity.

Who was Selena Ramirez—the woman, not just the doctor?

"This bread is delicious," she said. "I could make a meal of it. In fact, I probably shouldn't have ordered pasta. The salad would have been plenty."

"You can always take the leftovers home."

"That's true. I can eat it for lunch tomorrow, along with the chicken soup."

As she reached for her wineglass, he wondered what she thought about the setting he'd chosen. Did she suspect that he had ulterior motives by bringing her here?

Heck, he was wondering the same thing. Why *had* he chosen this place? And when had the desire to "pick her brain" about surrogacy issues morphed into a longing to know her better on a personal level?

On top of that, there was another question that concerned him even more. Why did the idea of kissing her again keep cropping up? Was there something going on in his subconscious that only his libido was privy to?

That might be the case, because for some darn reason, he wanted a chance to show her that he had a lot more up his sleeve than sweet goodnight kisses.

But getting involved with Selena—or any woman at this point in his life—would only complicate his plan to give those embryos a chance at life.

"I have a question for you," Selena said. "Why did Jim Ragsdale want to talk to you about his plans to use hippotherapy at the wellness center?"

"Because I know a lot about horses and can train them for him."

She leaned forward, her expressive gaze zeroing in on him. "So you raise horses on your ranch?"

He wondered what she found so intriguing—the fact that he owned a ranch in the first place or that he didn't raise cattle like most ranchers in these parts.

"Are you interested in hippotherapy?" he asked. "Or do you just like horses?"

"Both. I find the whole idea of using a horse's movements as therapy interesting. And I've always loved horses. As a girl, I dreamed of having one of my own, but we lived in a small house with very little yard. And even if we'd had a bigger place, my folks had a hard enough time feeding seven kids."

"Seven?" Alex, who'd been an only child, could hardly imagine what it would've been like to grow up in a family that large. "Where did you fit into the lineup?"

"I was the fourth child and the second daughter."

"Sounds to me as if it was pretty easy to get lost in the crowd."

She laughed. "That just about sums it up. Our family was loud and boisterous, and someone was always trying to be top dog."

"So there was some sibling rivalry going on."

"Some, but not as much as you'd think. We might have each gone out of our way to make our own mark, but we loved each other. And we've always been supportive."

"You undoubtedly studied hard, excelled in school and became a doctor. Your parents must be proud of you."

"They're proud of *all* of us. My sister Lucia is an award-winning graphic artist, and Diego graduated from West Point and is a lieutenant in the army." Selena sat back and smiled. "Let's see, there's a high school guidance counselor, a third-grade teacher, and Carlitos, the youngest, is a starting running back at Oklahoma State. Even Maria, who disliked sitting in a classroom and refused to consider college, is doing great. She married her high school sweetheart right after graduation. And now she's the best wife and mother in all of Tomball, Texas."

Alex chuckled, along with Selena, until her laughter stilled, her smile faded and her brow furrowed.

"What's the matter?" he asked.

She looked up as though surprised by his question, then shook off whatever had stolen the light from her eyes. "Nothing's wrong. I was just…thinking about something."

"What's that?"

She paused for a moment, as if she might share it with him, then she shrugged. "It was just a random thought."

He had an urge to coax it out of her, but let it go. "So you all succeeded one way or another."

"Yes, and we have our parents to thank for that. They

encouraged us to try our best. And even when one of us struggled or failed, we never doubted their love or support for a minute."

"And no one rebelled?" Alex found that odd, especially with seven kids in the family.

"Not really. Our neighborhood was a bit rough, so we all had to deal with the occasional gang- and drug-related issues. Carlitos, my little brother, gave them a few sleepless nights, but the older boys took him aside and let him know there'd be hell to pay if he gave my folks any trouble. And apparently, they made their point. He's doing really well now—in the classroom and on the football field."

For a moment, Alex thought about the babies he planned to raise, the kids who would depend on him for love and support. Would he prove to be the kind of father that Selena had? Would his children grow up to be happy and successful?

He certainly hoped so.

"I know I'm repeating myself," Alex said, "but your parents must be incredibly proud."

"Actually, we're just as proud of them as they are of us. They were both Mexican immigrants who didn't have a high school diploma. Instead, they had to work during their teen years to help support their families. But they were smart enough to know an education was the key to their kids' success."

It was probably safe to assume that her parents had some kind of blue-collar or service jobs, and while it really didn't matter, he couldn't quell his curiosity. "What did they do for a living?"

"My dad was a janitor at the elementary school near our house. And my mom cleaned houses. They were determined to cash in on the American dream and eventually bought a small, modest tract home in a better neighborhood."

The waiter returned with their meals at that point, and for a few minutes they ate in relative silence.

Then Alex's thoughts drifted back to her love of horses as a young girl and her wish to have one of her own. "So when was the last time you rode a horse?"

Selena looked up from her pasta primavera and smiled. "Not since high school. When I was a freshman, one of my girlfriends would invite me over for the weekend. Sometimes we'd go for a ride—when she wasn't competing in gymkhana."

Alex was familiar with the equestrian event she was talking about, which included barrel and flag racing, as well as other competitions that required teamwork between the horse and rider.

"She was really good," Selena added, "and I enjoyed watching her."

"It's too bad you didn't have a horse of your own."

"I would have been happy to have a dog, but that was out of the question, too." Selena glanced down at the table, those lush dark lashes drawing his attention, even without the use of mascara.

For a moment, he forgot that she was a doctor with a busy practice, that she probably was on call most weekends and that it was unlikely that the two of them would ever become more than friends.

"You ought to come out to my ranch someday," he said. "I'd let you ride one of my horses."

She looked up, emotion filling her eyes, making them glimmer in the candlelight. "Are you kidding?"

When she looked at him like that—with wonder splashed across her pretty face, the hope, the awe…

Hell, he'd never joke with her about anything that was special or important to her. "When is your next day off?"

"Sunday."

"Do you have plans?"

"Only to do laundry, pick up groceries for the week and maybe go to the wellness center and work out."

"Why don't you drive out to my place instead?" He watched her vacillate between an OMG-type response and a thanks-but-I'd-better-pass.

What was holding her back?

"I haven't been on a horse in ages," she finally said. "I probably wouldn't remember what to do."

"I've heard it's like riding a bicycle."

She laughed. "I haven't done that in a long time either—unless, of course, you count the stationary bike at the wellness center. I'd probably fall off a two-wheeler."

Right now, he was struggling to keep his own balance. Just the thought of showing Selena around—maybe saddling Sugar Foot, one of the gentler old mares—and taking her on a tour of the ranch had slapped a big old grin on his face. "I'm sure you'll do fine."

When she didn't challenge him, he figured she was leaning toward a yes. He sure hoped that was the case.

"Why don't you come out around nine or ten?" he suggested.

"Are you sure about that?"

"Absolutely. It'll be fun to take a pleasure ride for a change."

While they continued to eat their meals, he gave her directions to his ranch, as well as his cell phone number in case she got lost—or needed to make a change of plans.

He sure hoped nothing came up because he was looking forward to having her on his home turf.

After the waiter brought the bill and Alex paid with a credit card, he took Selena back to the wellness center, where she'd left her car. And once again, in spite of his plan to take things slow and not complicate his family plan, he got out of his truck and walked with her to her vehicle, telling himself he was just being polite.

But the fact was, he wanted to kiss her good-night again. And the silvery moon overhead wasn't making it any easier to walk away without doing what seemed to be natural at the end of a romantic evening.

Trouble was, a sweet, goodnight kiss might be considered appropriate, but that wasn't the kind he was tempted to give her.

So now what?
He thought it over for as long as he dared to.
Aw, what the hell…

Chapter Five

Selena had sensed that a kiss was coming the moment Alex had climbed out of his car. She'd felt it in the soft glimmer of moonlight, heard it in the crunch of his boots on the dusty pavement. And she'd seen it sparkle in his eyes—even before he reached for her waist, drew her close and placed his mouth on hers.

She could have taken a step back to let him know she wasn't interested—and she probably should have. Yet she didn't do one darn thing to avoid it. Instead, she leaned into him and slipped her arms around him as well.

Their first kiss had been sweet, tentative. But there was something bolder about this one, something decisive.

As their lips parted, as their tongues touched, Selena's common sense slipped by the wayside, and she kissed him right back—just as bold, just as decisive.

Within a heartbeat, the kiss deepened. Their breaths mingled, their tongues mated.

Had any man ever tasted so good, smelled so musky, felt so right in her arms?

As her pulse rate soared, her imagination took flight. Did she dare tiptoe around romance again?

Of course, wasn't she doing that now? Stepping out on a romantic limb, testing, pretending, wondering...

She had no idea what was really going on between her and Alex. And God only knew what tomorrow might hold, but there was no disputing the fact that something other than friendship was brewing between them.

And while she might go home tonight and regret that she'd let things come to this, she was determined to enjoy every sweet moment, every heated sensation now.

When Alex slowly drew back, allowing them both to come up for air, he placed his hand on her cheek and grinned. But Selena didn't dare return his smile. Instead, she stood there awestruck.

Who would have ever guessed that the handsome cowboy who'd sat in the front row of her lecture could kiss like that?

But as she took a deep, fortifying breath, reality chased away her romantic musing. She took a step back, desperate to regain her footing.

"I'll see you Sunday morning at nine," he said, as if

that's all there was to it. But things had taken a complicated turn, and there was so much more to consider.

"I don't have boots," she said, scurrying for some kind of excuse, some way to backpedal.

"Sneakers are fine. Don't worry about it."

But she *was* worried. And not just about what to wear or staying balanced in the saddle. She was worried about letting Alex think there was something between them, some kind of future.

Now wait a minute. It's not as if they'd actually gone out on a real date. Or if he'd asked her to do anything other than drive out to his ranch and go horseback riding.

Sure, the kiss had thrown her for a loop. And so had the romantic dinner. But that didn't mean she couldn't take things one day at a time.

"If something comes up," she said, "I'll give you a call." Then she climbed in her car and closed the door. Once she'd backed out of the parking lot and drove to the exit, she glanced in her rearview mirror, taking in the sight of the alluring man standing near his truck, the rancher who'd invited her to go riding with him on Sunday.

She probably ought to call him after she got home and tell him that something unexpected had come up, that she'd been called in to cover for a colleague, that she had to...wash her hair.

But she had a feeling she wouldn't do that.

For some reason, she wanted to see his ranch on Sunday, to go for a ride. And she wanted to spend more time with him, even if she feared it might be the riskiest thing she'd ever done.

The memory of Selena's kiss followed Alex all the way back to his ranch. But then again, why wouldn't it? The beautiful doctor had set off an unexpected flurry of testosterone that had damn near turned him inside out.

He'd never expected things to escalate between them like that, and he had to admit that he was glad it had. For the first time in two years—or maybe much longer than that—he'd felt alive again.

After parking his truck near the barn, he headed for the sprawling ranch house and let himself inside, where a lazy fire burned in the stone hearth of the wood-paneled living room, with its colorful southwestern paintings and decor.

"Lydia?" he called, as he hung his hat on the hook by the door. "I'm home."

Moments later, his housekeeper swept into the room wearing a smile of relief. "Oh, good. I was getting worried about you."

"I'm sorry. Something unexpected came up."

"At the fertility lecture?"

"Afterward." Alex wouldn't mention anything about Selena just yet, so that would require some stretching of the truth. "I ran into a friend at the wellness center, and we had dinner together. So that 'quick bite' I'd said I would get in town took a lot longer than I'd expected."

"I'm glad to hear you finally took some time for yourself. You don't get out as much as you should." She glanced at the mantel, at the framed photograph that had been taken on Alex and Mary's wedding day, then looked away as if realizing she'd been caught.

Alex had been tempted to remove that picture on several occasions because it always seemed to dampen his mood. But the babies would need to know who their mother was, so keeping her image close would be a good way to do that.

"I can warm up that leftover pot roast," Lydia said. "That is, if you're still hungry."

"Thanks, but I had lasagna this evening, so I'm stuffed." He crossed the hardwood floor to the center of the room and took a seat on the beige leather sofa Mary had purchased just months before she died. It suited the rest of the decor, but he'd always preferred the comfy overstuffed sofa that had been there for years.

"How about some coffee?" Lydia asked. "It's fresh. And I made brownies earlier this afternoon."

Lydia hadn't always doted on him before—not that she'd ever been less than professional. But she was a widow herself, so she understood the pain and grief of losing a spouse unexpectedly.

After the accident, Lydia had become more nurturing than she'd been when Mary had first hired her. And then last spring, after her youngest daughter got married and moved to Austin, she'd really taken Alex under her wing.

But he really didn't mind. It had been a long time since he'd known a mother's love. His mom had died when he was thirteen, so he appreciated Lydia's maternal side. In fact, she'd become more than a household employee. She'd turned into a friend—and the only real family Alex had left.

"All right," he said, "I'll take you up on the coffee and brownies. Thanks."

Her grin brightened, and then she bustled off to the kitchen. When she returned, she carried a tray with two steaming mugs and a platter of the chocolate treats and set it on the glass-top coffee table.

"So how was the lecture?" she asked.

"It was somewhat helpful."

Lydia knew all about Alex's plan to hire a gestational carrier and to raise the children on his own. In fact, he suspected she was nearly as eager as he was to have little ones in the house. He was even considering the idea of hiring a new cook and housekeeper because Lydia would be the one watching over the babies while he worked on the ranch.

"I expect to learn more next Tuesday," he added.

Of course, Selena had given him a list of agencies that might help him find someone to carry the babies. To be honest, it had nearly slipped his mind. He hadn't thought much about Mary or their future children today, even during the lecture. He'd been too caught up in watching the lovely doctor at the lectern—and then later, in the candlelight.

He wondered what Lydia would think of Selena when they met on Sunday. Not that it mattered, he supposed, but his housekeeper had gotten pretty protective over the past few months. Still, he imagined she'd be just as taken by the lovely doctor as he'd been.

Taken?

He blew out a ragged sigh, then reached for one of the mugs from the tray on the coffee table. He'd made a promise to his late wife that he intended to keep. But it wasn't just the promise prodding him to move forward. Having those children was something he needed to do. Somewhere down the road, Mary's obsession had become his own. And he wanted those babies—whether they were girls or boys, red-haired like she was, or blond like him.

God willing, he'd keep his vow to Mary, the deathbed promise he'd made to do all in his power to give their children a chance to live.

Alex had no idea what the future held for him and Selena, although he really liked the direction things were headed. For the first time in what seemed like forever, he found himself smiling for no reason at all.

Okay, so there actually was a reason—the memory of Selena sitting across a table from him, flashing him a pretty, dimpled smile.

He could imagine them dating and growing closer—both physically and emotionally.

Of course, he didn't know how she felt about dating a man who planned to hire a gestational carrier or what she thought about being involved with the pregnancy as well as the birth. Because if he went that route, he couldn't think of a better doctor to use.

But what about him? Did he even want to think about a romantic relationship at a time like this?

He hadn't even considered it until he'd met Selena, until he'd kissed her and held her in his arms.

It might be all right, though. Maybe even better than all right—just as long as she understood his desire to raise his and Mary's babies. If she did, then maybe they could give the whole relationship thing a whirl.

And if she couldn't?

Then all bets were off.

Alex hadn't taken time to call any of the agencies on the list Selena had given him Tuesday. However, on Saturday night, after dinner, he'd checked out each one on the internet. In fact, one in particular caught his eye.

Family Solutions was located in Wexler, so it was close. And if he was going to hire a gestational carrier, he liked the idea of knowing she lived nearby. He also liked the things he read on the website. In fact, he'd been so impressed that he'd sent an email asking for more information and had filled out a short questionnaire. At the end, it asked, Who can we thank for the referral, and Alex typed in: Dr. Selena Ramirez.

With that out of the way, he'd gone to sleep, eager to wake the next morning, when Selena would arrive at the ranch.

The day dawned bright, and he found himself looking forward to a long, leisurely ride with the lovely doctor.

He'd just poured his second cup of coffee and sat

down to look over the Sports page in the Sunday paper when she arrived. The moment he'd heard her car drive up, he got up from the kitchen table, went to the sink, where he poured out his cup. Then he went to greet her.

As he swung open the door, he found her standing on the porch, a shy smile on her pretty face. Her hair had been pulled back and woven in a single braid that hung down her back, her makeup applied lightly, her lipstick a pretty and kissable shade of pink.

He made a quick scan over the length of her, wishing he could allow his gaze to linger. In spite of claiming that she didn't have any boots, she'd obviously found a pair. She also wore jeans that hugged her hips and a lightweight knit top that caressed her curves.

He was going to have a tough time keeping his thoughts on horses, leisurely rides and the countryside.

"Do you think I'll need a jacket?" she asked.

"That's up to you. It's going to warm up soon."

Heck, it was warming up already. Somehow, over-night, Selena had morphed from a lovely, soft-spoken doctor to a sexy cowgirl. And he had no idea how that had happened.

It didn't matter, he supposed. Just as long as she was here.

"Would you like some breakfast?" he asked. "Or maybe a cup of coffee?"

"No, thanks. I've already eaten."

"Good. Then I'll take you out to meet Sugar Foot, a mare I think you'll like."

But before taking a step outside, a voice sounded

from behind him. "Don't forget your lunch, Mr. Connor."

Alex turned to see Lydia standing in the wings, no doubt waiting for an introduction. Why had she referred to him as mister? They'd been on a first-name basis ever since she'd come to work for him and Mary.

"Lydia," he said, moving aside so his housekeeper could greet his guest, "this is Selena…or rather, Dr. Ramirez."

Selena offered Lydia a warm smile and extended her arm in greeting. "Let's not be formal. Please call me Selena."

Lydia took the pretty doctor's hand and gave it a gentle shake, gracefully moving from loyal employee to family friend. "It's nice to meet you."

Before either woman could turn a casual introduction into a longer chat, Alex said, "I'll take Selena with me so she can meet her horse. Before we ride out, we'll stop by the kitchen and pick up our lunch."

Then he stepped onto the porch, joining Selena and starting toward the barn, where he'd stabled the two horses he'd planned for them to ride.

"Thanks again for inviting me out to the ranch," she said.

"I'm glad you came. To be honest, you're doing me a favor. I haven't taken the time to ride just for the fun of it in a long time. And it looks like today will be the perfect day for it." He wasn't just talking about the mild temperature or the warmth of the sun either.

As they crossed the yard toward the barn, Gus Barrows, one of the ranch hands, came ambling toward them. He was leading a bay gelding with one hand and had a red bandana tied around the other.

"What did you do to yourself?" Alex asked.

The gruff fifty-something cowboy let out a huff, then slowly shook his head. "I cut my dad-burn hand on a piece of twisted metal on one of the corral gates. I thought I'd better come in and put a real bandage on it before going back to work."

"Do you mind if I take a look at that?" Selena asked.

"It ain't nothing." Still, Gus lifted his hand and unwrapped the cloth from his palm, where a cut ran jagged and deep.

As Selena looked at his injury, her pretty face scrunched in concern. "That cut is severe. You might have damaged a tendon. And even if you didn't, it's not going to heal without stitches."

"Aw, it ain't so bad." Gus slowly drew his hand back.

"When was your last tetanus shot?" she asked.

"I don't know. When I was a kid, I suppose."

Selena glanced at Alex, her expression filled with unspoken words, each one coaxing him to put his foot down and insist that Gus seek medical attention.

"I'll ask Lydia to drive you to the urgent care," Alex said.

"That ain't necessary, boss. If you want me to have it checked out, I can drive my…" Gus glanced at the house, and his expression softened. "Well, maybe it would be best if Lydia took me. That is, if you don't think she'd mind."

Alex had noticed a starry-eyed look in Gus's eyes once or twice when the housekeeper had been in sight. Maybe Gus would appreciate a little feminine TLC for a change.

"I'm sure you can drive yourself into town," Alex said, "but I'd feel better if someone took you. And the only one available today, since it's Sunday, is Lydia."

"If you think she wouldn't mind…"

"I'm sure she'd be happy to." Besides, it would give her someone else to fuss over for a change.

"Okay, then," Gus said. "Maybe I ought to go and… you know, wash up."

A grin tugged at Alex's lips. "Sure. You do that. And I'll tell Lydia you'll be waiting by her car."

As the rough and tough old cowboy headed for the bunkhouse, leaving Alex and Selena standing in the middle of the yard, Alex nodded toward the house. "If you'll give me a moment, I'll let Lydia know what's going on."

"No problem."

Moments later, while Lydia went hunting for her purse and the keys to her car, Alex returned to Selena. While he'd been in the house, she'd wandered over to the corral nearest the barn, where Lady Gwen grazed with her foal.

"I'm sorry to keep you waiting."

Selena turned to him, her eyes wide and sparkling. "I didn't mind."

He didn't suppose she did. She might have grown up and gone to medical school, but she still loved horses.

And the sparkle in her eye was doing something to him, especially because her visit to his ranch had put it there. Or was something else happening?

They stood like that for a moment, gazes locked, attraction flaring—at least on his part. And while he was tempted to ease forward, to cross some platonic line that remained between them in spite of two kisses that had been a little more than friendly, he couldn't let things get out of hand yet. So he shook it off and said, "Come on, let's go saddle our horses."

Once inside the barn, he led her to the stall of his favorite broodmare, a roan filly that was gentle enough for an inexperienced rider. "This little gal is Sugar Foot."

Selena reached out and stroked the horse's nose. "Hi, there, Sugar. It's nice to meet you."

The mare gave a little whinny, and Selena broke into a beautiful smile that stirred up something warm in Alex's heart.

He watched the woman and the mare for a moment, then leaned against the rails of the stall. "So what do you think? She's a good horse—and gentle. I can find one with more spunk, if you'd rather."

"Oh, no. I like Sugar Foot. I think we'll get along just fine." As she smiled, her eyes lit up, making her look younger than she probably was—early to mid-thirties.

He could imagine her as a teenager again, eagerly preparing to mount her friend's horse, dreaming it was her own. And he was glad he'd been able to offer her something special, an afternoon she was sure to enjoy.

He was glad for himself, too. This was the first time

he'd met a woman who'd taken his mind off his loss. He actually enjoyed the time he'd spent with Selena. Maybe that meant his heart was on the mend.

And that the shadow of guilt that had dogged him these past two years would finally lift.

"Okay," he said, "let's get her saddled for you."

Ten minutes later, he'd saddled both Sugar Foot and a roan gelding he'd just acquired, along with several others, at auction last week. Because he'd wanted to try him out, he figured today was as good a day as any.

"What's his name?" Selena asked, as she stroked the roan's neck.

"I don't remember. Bailey something or other." Alex stole a glance at Selena, saw her brow furrowed as she processed his response. For some reason, even though his spread numbered in the hundreds and he couldn't remember each horse by name, he didn't like knowing that she was bothered by it.

"He's registered with the American Quarter Horse Association," he explained, "so he has an official name. But we've been calling him Bailey for short." At least, that would be his nickname now.

Her expression lifted at that, apparently pleased that the new horse wasn't merely one of hundreds when that actually was the case.

After leading the horses out of the barn, they stopped near the service porch, which was at the back of the house, just off the kitchen.

"Wait here," Alex said, leaving Selena to hold both sets of reins. Then he went inside, just long enough to pick up the knapsack Lydia had packed with their lunch, as well as a small checkered tablecloth on which they could set out their picnic.

When he returned, he helped Selena mount, giving her a foot up. She might be dressed like a cowgirl, yet her scent—something soft and floral—whispered "Lady" through and through.

As she climbed into her saddle, her denim-clad derriere rising to his eye level, he tried to ignore the growing attraction to the lovely doctor to no avail.

Once she was mounted, he climbed onto his own horse, sitting a bit taller in the saddle than he had in recent months, or maybe even in recent years. And as they headed out, his heart soared at the thought of leaving it all behind—the house, the chores, the daily grind.

But more than that, he seemed to have finally—or at least, temporarily—shaken that dark shadow of grief and guilt that plagued him more often than not.

As the sun stretched high over the cloud-speckled Texas sky, Alex and Selena continued a leisurely ride, following the creek that ran through his property to a small lake surrounded by cottonwood trees, where they slowed to a stop.

"This is where I learned to fish and to swim," Alex told her.

"I can't imagine what it would have been like to grow up on a ranch like this. It would have been a dream come true for me." Having been raised in a small desert town in New Mexico, where trees and streams and swimming holes didn't even exist, other than in travel magazines or books in the library, Selena relished the sight of the lush green pastures and the horses grazing with their foals, as well as the scent of fertile ground that mingled with the hint of autumn.

"Then I'm glad I was able to share this with you."

She stole a glance at Alex, saw him leaning forward in the saddle, his hands resting on the pommel. The man had an amazing profile and an even more remarkable build—lean, strong and as sexy as they came.

His black Stetson shielded his eyes from the sun, but not from her. As their gazes met and locked, something sparked between them—something more powerful than she'd expected, more alluring.

"Come on," Alex said, breaking eye contact and drawing her from her musing. "I'm sure you're getting hungry. I certainly am. And I know the perfect place to eat."

She'd had a light breakfast this morning because she'd been plagued by nerves. But they'd dissipated the moment she and Alex had struck out on their ride, so she was more than ready for a lunch break. "All right. That sounds like a good idea."

They continued on for another twenty minutes or so, following a trail that led up a mountain—or maybe it was more of a hillside.

"We call this summit Ol' Piney," he said.

We? Had he brought his wife here?

Well, of course, he had. Why wouldn't he have done that? It was beautiful.

"My uncle was the first to bring me out here, and that's what he called it."

Selena studied the pine trees that lined the trail, reminding her of a view one might see on a postcard.

"Let's eat here," he said, as he swung off his horse. "It has a great view of the valley."

Again, she thought of his late wife because she couldn't imagine him and his uncle having picnics together. She wasn't sure what bothered her about the idea. After all, the poor woman was dead and gone.

But the fact that Alex had cared so deeply for her, that he planned to utilize the embryos they'd created together and raise them himself, left her uneasy and even a bit sad. The woman who was destined to become Alex's second wife would have to compete with Mary Connor's memory, and Selena wasn't up for the task.

Besides, she really wasn't interested in dating Alex. Not really. They'd merely struck up a friendship—at least, so far.

"Can I help you down?" Alex asked, as he approached her horse.

She figured she could make it on her own, but for some silly reason, she liked the idea of letting the handsome cowboy help her dismount. "All right."

As she held the reins and gripped the pommel, she pulled her foot from the stirrup and swung her leg over the saddle.

Alex reached for her. As his hands wrapped around her waist, setting off tremors of heat to her core, her breath caught.

The moment her feet touched the ground, her legs wobbled. She wasn't sure if her unsteadiness was due to her reaction to his touch and his rugged cowboy scent, both of which sent her senses reeling, or whether it was from being in the saddle so long. Either way, the combination was doing a real number on her.

He continued to hold her steady, which was a good thing, because she'd hate to collapse on the ground in a heap. As she slowly turned to face him, his hands remained loosely at her waist, setting off a flutter in her heart.

As their gazes met and held, her pulse spiked, and for a moment, she thought he was going to kiss her.

Yes, she thought. Her heart hammered in anticipation, and her breathing nearly stopped. Yet instead of slipping his arms around her, drawing her close and placing his lips on hers, he slowly eased back.

Why hadn't he taken the opportunity while he'd had it?

And why did she find his reluctance so disheartening?

"Come here," he said, dropping the reins and heading toward a large rock. "I want to show you something."

What could he possibly think she'd find more interesting than a kiss? And why had he released the gelding's reins? Wasn't he worried it would run off?

"What about the horses?" she asked.

"Let them graze."

As Selena released the reins, allowing Sugar Foot

to lower her head and nibble on the grass, she followed Alex to the rock where he stood.

He pointed to the valley below, where a small town lay nestled against the trees. Thanks to the arrival of autumn, the leaves were a kaleidoscope of fall shades—rust, red, yellow and the occasional green.

"It's Brighton Valley," she said, scanning the small buildings and houses and noting the steeple of the community church. "It looks different from up here, doesn't it?"

He pointed to the east. "That's Main Street and the old part of town."

She nodded, spotting the cars parked along the storefronts.

"Now look to the west, just beyond the medical center. On a clear day, you can even see Wexler."

"It's an amazing view from up here. It looks like something you'd find on a postcard."

"I thought you'd like it."

She studied the quaint and colorful scene a moment longer, then turned to him and smiled. "Thank you."

"For what? Bringing you to Ol' Piney?"

"For everything—the ride, the tour of your ranch, the lovely view…"

"I'm glad you're having fun."

It was more than fun. She'd been waiting for this day since the moment he'd invited her to come out to the ranch, yet it was more than the outdoors and horseback riding she'd been dreaming about. But she didn't dare let on about that.

"Are you ready to eat?" he asked.

"Sure."

Yet he didn't make a move to get their lunch out of the knapsack. Instead, he remained in front of her, face-to-face. An arm's distance apart.

His gaze held an intensity that set her heart on edge again. And she sensed another kiss coming her way. But this time, she didn't want to risk the chance of him drawing away, like he did just moments ago. So she did something she might regret later.

She reached up, slipped her arms around his neck and drew his mouth to hers.

Chapter Six

Alex hadn't expected Selena to make the first move, but he was glad that she had. He'd been dying to wrap his arms around her all day, and it was nice to know that he wasn't the only one caught up in a growing sexual attraction and succumbing to temptation.

As their mouths met, her lips parted, inviting him to be an active participant. And that's just what he did. He kissed her as if there were no tomorrow, as if there were every reason in the world for them to be lovers—and nothing waiting in the wings to hold them back.

And maybe there wasn't. She'd known what he planned to do. And she'd still instigated the kiss.

Didn't that mean she'd be on the same page with him when it came to hiring a woman to carry the embryos to term?

Of course the answer to that question, as well as his baby plan, quickly dissipated in the heat of the moment.

As Selena leaned into him, pressing her breasts against his chest, their bodies melded together as if they were meant for each other. And right now, Alex didn't have any reason to doubt that they hadn't been.

While they continued to kiss, he ran his hands along her back, exploring the slope of her hips, caressing each feminine curve. As he relished the feel of her in his arms, he savored her taste and her soft floral scent until his hormones spun out of control.

What he wouldn't give to have her back at the ranch house with him at this very minute, with music playing in the background, a fire in the hearth, candles lit, the coverlet pulled back on the bed in readiness.

But he wasn't at home. They were several miles away, in an outdoor world of their own making.

So what was he supposed to do here and now? Stretch that tablecloth across the ground for them to use in lieu of a king-size bed?

While tempted to do just that, he slowly drew back, breaking the kiss and allowing them both to come up for air. Still, his heart was pounding like a son of a gun, and his blood continued to rush through his veins.

She looked up at him with an expression that asked, *Where do we go from here?*

He'd be damned if he knew, especially when he had no idea how she'd feel about raising another woman's babies. And that's something Selena would have to consider doing if they took the whole idea of a relationship any further than this.

But it was too soon to discuss a complex future between them like that, especially because he would begin to earnestly search for a gestational carrier soon.

Or would Selena be willing to carry the babies for him?

It was a lot to ask a woman, especially one who hadn't had any children of her own yet.

For a moment, he envisioned having a baby the old-fashioned way—by making love with Selena and then watching her belly grow with a child they'd created. The thought, while warm and tender, wasn't one he could consider. Not when he still had those embryos waiting to be born.

Besides, it was far too early at this stage of their budding relationship to even broach a subject like that, so he decided to focus on something else, something other than a burning sexual desire that could very easily lead to broken promises and shattered dreams.

"Are you ready for lunch?" he asked, deciding to make light of it for now.

She blinked, then blinked a second time as if she was having trouble distancing her physical hunger from a sexual one. And he couldn't blame her one bit for that. Hell, that's exactly what was going on with him. He was drowning in a flood of testosterone, grasping for straws that made sense, desperate with longing…

And hungry for a hell of a lot more than the sandwiches Lydia had made them.

But there was no way he could let Selena know all that.

How could he when he didn't know if his attraction to her was only a passing fancy? So he strode toward Bailey, reached for the knapsack he'd secured to the saddle and untied it. "I'll water the horses if you'd like to set out the food."

As he handed the canvas sack to her, he noted bewilderment splashed across her face.

"Would you rather I did it?" he asked. "I'll just be a minute or two."

She blinked again, clearly reeling from the kiss—or maybe from his reluctance to talk about it.

"No," she said softly, taking the knapsack from him. "I'll do it."

"There's a tablecloth inside," he said, as he returned to the horses.

She glanced at the bag that had been packed with their lunch, and when she broke eye contact with him, he collected the reins and started toward the creek with both horses.

Had he defused the situation? Or merely made things worse by leaving her confused and maybe a bit angry?

He was tempted to steal a glance over his shoulder, but he continued toward the stream instead.

Rather than spread the tablecloth on the ground and set out their lunches as Alex had asked her to do, Selena remained rooted to the spot where she stood, gaping at the man who'd just kissed her senseless, then shrugged it all off as if it were nothing and walked away.

How could he kiss her like that, turning her inside out, then pretend as if it had never happened, as if they didn't have to broach the subject of relationships, dating or even making love?

Her first thought was that it was just a matter of hormones and biology at work. After all, his wife had been gone for two years—unless he'd dated in the past, which she doubted. She had a feeling he might still be married in his heart, so he probably hadn't had sex in a long time.

Yet she couldn't ignore what had just happened between them. So she brought it out in the open. "What was that all about, Alex?"

His steps slowed to a stop and he turned to her. "What do you mean? The *kiss?*"

"For starters, yes."

A slow grin stretched across his face. "You made the first move this time. Maybe I should be the one asking the questions."

"You didn't fight it."

His grin deepened, and his eyes gleamed. "Only a fool would have done that, Selena."

She opened her mouth to object, then set the knapsack on the ground and crossed her arms instead. "Well, thanks for giving it the old college try."

"Wait a second. Are you upset?"

Of course she was upset. And embarrassed, too.

"Why?" he asked. "I thought you enjoyed it."

"I did. And unless you're a big fat liar, you did, too."

"Oh, there's no doubt about that."

"Then why did you just walk away as if it never happened?"

He stood there for a moment, holding the reins of the horses, then dropped his head. When he looked up, he said, "I'm sorry. I should have addressed it, I guess, but I wasn't sure what to say. A part of me wanted to ask if you'd ever made love outdoors."

She hadn't. And with that kiss still fresh in her mind, she thought the whole idea sounded…intriguing. And far more tempting than she could have imagined. But she had to get something other than the vision of their bare bodies out in the open.

"What's going on between us?" she asked, determined to learn what he thought, what he might feel.

"I'm not sure." His smile faded, and his expression grew serious. "There's definitely a strong sexual attraction between us. And some genuine feelings. But to be honest, I'm not sure what to do about it at this stage of the game."

She arched a brow.

"Well, let me rephrase that. I know *exactly* what to do about it, but I'm not sure if that would be wise."

Her arms loosened and slowly uncrossed. "I'm reluctant to get involved with you, too. But what's holding you back?"

He paused for the longest time, as if he wasn't sure if he wanted to reveal his concerns or not. Then he said, "I'd like nothing more than to date you and to see where things go. But I have some things I need to do. And I'm not sure..."

"If I'd fit into those plans?"

Again he pondered his answer for a beat. "No, it's not that. You'd fit in nicely. But I'm not sure how you'd feel about dating a single father, which is what I plan to be within the next year if things work out."

The embryos. His plan to have his late wife's children.

Selena might be dealing with a growing attraction to Alex, but part of that was curiosity and maybe even envy. What she wouldn't give to find a man who'd love her in the way Alex had obviously loved his wife.

And look what she'd just done. She'd stepped out on a limb and kissed him.

But how could she not? He was far more tempting than he ought to be. If things were different, she could easily fall for a man like Alex, but that would lock her into a second-place role she couldn't and wouldn't accept.

So she unfolded her arms and reached for the knapsack on the ground. "You're right. It's a complex situation. And we really need to take things slowly." That is, if they took things anywhere at all.

"I'm glad you understand."

Sadly, she did. "You have a family waiting to be born."

"Are you okay with that?" he asked.

To be honest? "I'm not sure."

The whole idea of dating a single dad was one thing.

She would actually end up having children and a family that way. But in this case, she'd be playing second fiddle to his wife's memory and to the children they'd planned to raise together before that tragic accident left Alex heartbroken and alone. So it wasn't the same thing at all.

"Let's just take things one day at a time," she said. "Is that all right with you?"

Alex's smile sent Selena's heart hurtling through her chest as though it might disintegrate upon landing. "Okay, that's fair enough."

Then he turned and walked the horses to the creek.

But it wasn't okay. And it wasn't the least bit fair. The last thing in the world Selena needed to do was to fall for a man whose heart would always belong to someone else.

The picnic they shared—Dagwood sandwiches, oranges and homemade chocolate chip cookies—was tasty. And while they'd kept the mealtime conversation light, the memory of that arousing kiss remained on Selena's mind for the rest of the afternoon.

Was Alex thinking about it, too?

She couldn't see how he wouldn't be, even though he appeared to have shut it out of his mind as if it had never happened. She probably ought to consider skirting emotional issues to be a fault of his, yet there was something about Alex she found appealing. And she couldn't help forgiving him for that weakness.

Would she ever meet another man like him someday? She certainly hoped so. She'd have to make it a point to get out in the real world more often so she would have more opportunities for romance.

Of course, she'd certainly gotten out of the office and away from the medical center today. Riding with Alex, seeing his beautiful ranch and breathing in the fresh air had been invigorating—and just what she'd needed. There was something to the old "all work and no play" adage.

She'd probably be sore tomorrow from her time spent in the saddle, but she didn't care. The day had been amazing so far, and she was sorry to see the sun descending in the west Texas sky.

When they returned to the ranch and rode into the yard, a young cowboy wearing a black felt hat, a red plaid shirt and jeans met them and approached Alex. "Hey, boss. If you're done with those horses, I can take them for you."

"What are you doing here?" Alex asked, as he dismounted. "This is your day off, Troy."

"Yeah, I know, but Lydia called and asked me to cover for Gus. She took him to the urgent care in town, only they sent him to the hospital. I guess he did a real number on his hand. He's having surgery this afternoon."

Selena had suspected the ranch hand's cut had reached the tendons, so she was glad the housekeeper had taken him to have it checked.

"Lydia's still at the hospital," Troy added. "She plans to stay there until Gus gets out of recovery."

"I really appreciate your coming out here on such

short notice," Alex told the cowboy. "I'm sorry if it interfered with any plans you might have had."

"I was just going to shoot a little pool down at the Stagecoach Inn, but it's not a problem. Gus would have done the same for me." Troy glanced at Selena, then back at Alex. "So what do you say, boss? Do you want me to cool down those horses for you?"

"Sure, that would be great." Alex handed over his reins, then he made his way to Sugar Foot's side and reached up to help Selena down.

She was glad they had an audience. It might make being in Alex's arms a little less awkward, a little less tempting. So she carefully removed her foot from the stirrup, then lifted her leg over the saddle.

Alex reached for her, setting off a shiver of arousal through her bloodstream. So much for avoiding any awkward feelings and urges.

"Why don't you come inside for a while?" Alex asked. "Lydia probably has some iced tea or lemonade made. I can even open a beer or a bottle of wine, if you'd like."

She pondered the wisdom of accepting his invitation, but only for a moment, because it seemed that he wasn't ready to say goodbye. And for some fool reason, neither was she.

"Actually," she said, brushing her hands against her denim-clad hips, "something thirst-quenching sounds great."

"You got it. Come on in."

Selena followed Alex to the back door of the house,

entering through the service porch, where they both washed up at the utility sink. Then he led her to a tidy kitchen, which had been painted a rusted red color.

It was a nice room, she decided, functional and newly remodeled, with gray faux-marble countertops, a fairly new stainless steel stove and oven, as well as a built-in refrigerator.

Someone had gone all out on decorating the room that was central to any house. Had it been Lydia, the housekeeper?

Or had Alex's late wife been the one to create an efficient place to cook and to eat?

"Why don't you have a seat?" Alex indicated a round oak table that Selena suspected was an antique—the only thing in the room that wasn't modern and new. "I'll get our drinks."

As Selena pulled out one of the chairs, she noted the scarred wood tabletop as well as a vase that bore a bouquet of multicolored roses.

"We're in luck," Alex said. "There's sun tea on the counter as well as fresh lemonade in the fridge. Which would you prefer?"

"Lemonade," she said.

As she watched him take a pitcher from the refrigerator, glasses from the cupboard and ice cubes from the freezer, she realized she'd have to use the bathroom sooner or later, especially if she had anything to drink. So she asked him where she could find the nearest one.

"Just go through the doorway into the living room.

You'll see a hallway near the fireplace. The guest bathroom is the first door on the right."

She thanked him, then followed his directions, pausing long enough to study the cozy living area, with its beige-colored walls, dark wood beams and a stone fireplace. Like the kitchen, the decor in this room also bore the markings of a woman's hand—like the red knit throw that draped over the back and the armrest of a beige leather sofa, the floral watercolor artwork, the crystal figurines on the mantel.

Unable to help herself, Selena wandered to the fireplace, where several framed pictures were displayed. She would have checked them all out, but one in particular drew her complete attention—a wedding photo of Alex and his late wife.

Mary Connor was a pretty bride, a wholesome redhead with a scatter of freckles across her nose and a starry-eyed smile. Alex, stunningly handsome in a tuxedo and a black bow tie, appeared to be just as happy.

A pang of sadness pierced Selena's heart. Alex had lost the woman he'd vowed to love for as long as they both would live. And the fact that he kept that photo in such a prominent position on the mantel was proof that he'd never forgotten her, even two years after her unexpected death.

Was he destined to love her even beyond that?

Selena couldn't help but think that he was, and at that realization, apprehension flared and she was forced to face the inevitable. If Alex ever married again, his new wife would always have to compete with the woman he'd lost.

Selena continued to study the picture longer than she should have, imagining the beautiful children the couple would have produced—the children he would actually have if he went through with his plan to hire a woman to carry those embryos to term.

And why shouldn't he? They were his future sons or daughters, conceived with eggs of the woman he loved.

Realizing that she'd lingered too long and afraid that Alex would wonder what was keeping her, she replaced the frame on the mantel, then hurried to the bathroom to do what she'd set out to do. All the while, she continued to think about Alex, about the heated kiss they'd shared while out on their ride. The kiss he'd tried to ignore.

He'd admitted to being aroused by it—and tempted to suggest that they make love.

The tone of his voice, his expression, insisted that he'd been telling the truth. So why did he just walk away as if it had never happened?

She'd asked him flat out, then held her breath, awaiting his answer. But his response had surprised her. He'd told her that he hadn't known what to say.

But why was that?

In spite of her disbelief and skepticism at the time, she'd told herself that he'd been so swept away by his desire for more than a kiss that he'd been speechless. But now she realized it was probably more than that. Maybe he'd felt guilty for kissing her—and even more so by his physical response to it and his desire for a sexual release.

Of course, he'd mentioned that a part of him had wanted to ask if she'd ever made love outdoors.

She hadn't, of course, done anything that bold before. But his question and her answer had only masked what he hadn't come out and said.

If a part of him had wondered about sex, what had the rest of him been thinking?

Rather than try to second guess his reservations, Selena turned on the water in the bathroom sink and reached for the soap, hoping to rid herself of the perplexing thoughts as easily as she washed any lingering trail dust from her hands.

One thing was for certain, though. A relationship with Alex wasn't in the cards for her. She'd already suffered a major breakup while in college, when her first love had gone home to visit during Christmas break, only to fall in love with his high school sweetheart all over again.

Why in the world would she want to set herself up for another failed romance?

She dried her hands on one of the fluffy blue towels hanging on the rack, then headed back to the kitchen where she'd left Alex and the lemonade.

She'd no more than reached the living room when she spotted Alex greeting his housekeeper at the front door.

"How's Gus doing?" Alex asked her.

"He came through the surgery just fine and is in the

recovery room now. So I headed home. I promised to come back and check on him tonight."

"It's a good thing Selena was here," Alex said, as he stepped aside to let Lydia in the house. "If she hadn't seen how serious that injury was, Gus probably wouldn't have let a doctor check it out."

Lydia, an attractive woman in her late forties to early fifties, slowly shook her head and clicked her tongue. "Can you believe it? That man complained about going to the E.R. all the way to Brighton Valley. He insisted that he didn't need any help, that he'd had worse injuries before."

"Gus has always been a tough old bird," Alex said.

"Tell me about it." Lydia placed her black handbag on the table by the door. "When the doctor in the emergency room told him he was going to need surgery, he argued with her for a while, telling her it would be just fine. But when she explained that he stood to lose the use of his hand, if not lose it altogether, he finally agreed. But he insisted that they do it as an outpatient procedure."

"What did the doctor say to that?"

"She referred him to a surgeon, who said he would have considered it, but Gus's blood pressure was high when we arrived. They ended up doing the surgery anyway, but they wanted to keep him overnight for observation."

"I'm glad they're being cautious." Alex closed the door, then joined Lydia in the living area. "Gus never mentioned anything about having high blood pressure to me."

"I'm sure he never even knew it. He told me that he hadn't seen a doctor since he'd been in the army back in the late seventies."

"Who did the surgery?" Selena asked, as she entered the living room and joined Alex and his housekeeper.

"Dr. Goldman," Lydia said. "Do you know him?"

"He's done some amazing work with hand injuries, so I'm glad Betsy was able to call him in."

"Betsy?" Lydia asked.

"Oh, I'm sorry. The only female doctor working in the ER at the medical center is Betsy Nielson-Alvarez."

"Yes, that's her. She was awesome. If I'm ever in need of an E.R. doctor, I hope she's on call. She was good with Gus, even though he was a lousy patient." Lydia plopped down on one of the overstuffed chairs in the living room. "I swear, Alex, I've never seen a more bullheaded man in my life. He probably drove his first wife crazy."

"He's never been married," Alex said.

"Well, that's too bad. A good woman might have put a smile on his face."

Alex laughed. "Maybe it's not too late for that."

Lydia studied her boss for a moment, their gazes speaking through the silence. Then she said, "I'm not so sure he'd be interested."

"You never know unless you try."

Lydia crossed her arms, and furrowed her brow, clearly pondering Alex's suggestion. Moments later, she looked up and grinned. "Maybe you're right. I think I'll pack up some of those chocolate chip cookies I made yesterday and take them to him when I go back to the hospital this evening."

As Lydia got to her feet and headed to the kitchen, Selena took the opportunity to escape the temptation to pursue what would only end up being a star-crossed relationship with Alex.

"I'm going to have to go," she said, as she crossed the hardwood floor to where Alex stood.

Selena's sudden announcement threw Alex for a moment, and he turned to her, stunned. "What about that lemonade?"

"I'm afraid I'll have to take a rain check. I just remembered a meeting I'd scheduled with a colleague. If I leave now, I'll make it just in time."

As Selena started for the front door, Alex followed her. "I'll walk you to the car."

She glanced over her shoulder. "You don't need to."

"I know, but I want to." And he did. He'd found himself increasingly drawn to the lovely obstetrician. She was bright and funny, compassionate and sweet.

And on top of that, the kisses they'd shared, especially the one up on Ol' Piney, had nearly knocked him to his knees. Of course, it also had him running a bit scared because getting involved with Selena might complicate the future he'd planned.

Okay, so he and Selena really hadn't gotten "involved" quite yet. But all afternoon he'd found himself comparing Selena to Mary, which wasn't fair to either of them.

Now, as he followed Selena out the front door and onto the veranda, he watched her pat the small bulge in the front pocket of her jeans, assuming it had been made by her car keys since she didn't have a purse with her.

"Thanks so much for inviting me out to the ranch today," she said as she made her way toward the barn where she'd parked her Lexus. "I really enjoyed that ride. It was a real treat for a wannabe cowgirl."

"I'm glad," he said, walking along with her. "I enjoyed it, too. I'd forgotten how nice it is to go on a ride just for the fun of it. You'll have to come out again—soon."

"Thank you." She smiled, yet her eyes had lost the spark they'd had earlier.

Had something happened between the time she'd agreed to have a glass of lemonade and Lydia's arrival? It sure seemed that way.

Or maybe she'd been telling the truth when she said that she'd just remembered an appointment she had. Maybe the talk about Gus and the surgery and the ER doctor had been a reminder of her meeting.

Yeah, that had to be it. He shook off his apprehension as they approached her vehicle.

"I wasn't kidding when I told you that you're always welcome here," he said, trying to stretch things out.

"I really appreciate that, Alex. You have a beautiful ranch. It's a great place to ride. And I really like Sugar Foot. She's the kind of horse I would have wanted when

I was a girl." Selena reached for the door handle on the driver's side and opened it.

He probably ought to just step back and let her go because they were both tiptoeing around the idea of a relationship—and for good reason. Yet his hormones seemed to have a mind of their own.

Instead of stepping back, he eased forward and placed a hand along her jaw. Then he brushed a good-bye kiss across her lips.

It was a gentle movement, a friendly way to end the day. And while he was sorely tempted to kiss her sense-less, he managed to hold himself in check.

"Drive carefully," he said.

"I will."

She hesitated for a moment, and his resolve to keep things simple, platonic and safe withered in the after-noon breeze.

As her fading floral scent snaked round him, bind-ing him to her somehow, his thumb brushed against her cheek.

Her eyes widened, and her lips parted, letting him know they were both fighting the same temptation. So he threw caution to the wind and kissed her the way he'd been dying to do since lunchtime.

Chapter Seven

As Alex leaned in to kiss Selena a second time, she should have stopped him, yet for some reason, against her better judgment, she wrapped her arms around him and kissed him right back.

How could she do anything else? After all, Alex had been right when he'd said only a fool would have fought their sexual attraction.

And while that might be true, Selena couldn't risk becoming a fool when it came to getting emotionally involved with a handsome rancher who hadn't gotten over his late wife—and probably never would.

Sure, biology and hormones might play in Selena's favor. Alex would eventually lower his guard and have sex again, either with her or with someone else. And she suspected that it would happen sooner rather than later.

Get 2 Books FREE!

Harlequin® Books,
publisher of women's fiction,
presents

Harlequin®

SPECIAL EDITION

GET 2 BOOKS

We'd like to send you two *Harlequin® Special Edition* novels absolutely free. Accepting them puts you under no obligation to purchase any more books.

HOW TO GET YOUR
2 FREE BOOKS AND 2 FREE GIFTS

1. Return the reply card today, and we'll send you two *Harlequin Special Edition* novels, absolutely free! We'll even pay the postage!

2. Accepting free books places you under no obligation to buy anything, ever. Whatever you decide, the free books and gifts are yours to keep, free!

3. We hope that after receiving your free books you'll want to remain a subscriber, but the choice is yours– to continue or cancel, any time at all!

EXTRA BONUS

You'll also get two free mystery gifts!
(worth about $10)

FREE!

Return this card today to get
2 FREE BOOKS and 2 FREE GIFTS!

 Harlequin®

SPECIAL EDITION

YES! Please send me 2 FREE *Harlequin® Special Edition*
novels, and 2 FREE mystery gifts as well. I understand
I am under no obligation to purchase anything, as
explained on the back of this insert.

235/335 HDL FMKU

Please Print

FIRST NAME	LAST NAME

ADDRESS

APT.#	CITY

STATE/PROV.   ZIP/POSTAL CODE

Visit us at:
www.ReaderService.com

▼ DETACH AND MAIL CARD TODAY! ▼

H-SE-03/12

But that didn't mean the woman who finally made love with him would win his undying devotion.

Sadly, it appeared that his first wife already had a lock on that.

So Selena placed her hands on his chest and gently pressed against him while drawing her lips from his.

It was the best thing to do, she told herself. Hadn't she already decided to end their harmless flirtation— or whatever it was—before it was too late to walk away without risking her heart?

Yet as they drew apart, she yearned for more of his taste, his touch, his scent.

Did he realize that ending things—and not just the kiss—was a real struggle for her?

Probably not, because a boyish grin tugged at his lips, and a glimmer lit his eyes.

"Kissing you is becoming a habit," he said.

A bad one, she feared. But why make a remark like that now? She'd already decided that she wasn't up for any heavy discussions, especially when she was determined to leave the ranch as quickly as possible.

But to clear up any false assumptions he might have made about what that goodnight kiss meant, she would have to lay it on the line.

"We talked about this earlier," she said. "Your future is going to be complicated enough without having to deal with a new relationship."

He seemed to ponder her comment for the longest time. With each second that passed, something in her chest gripped and tightened, squeezing the breath right out of her.

Why didn't he argue with her and tell her that she was wrong?

He couldn't, of course, because they both knew the truth.

"About those embryos," he said, getting right to the heart of the matter.

When he didn't immediately finish what he'd started to say, she was tempted to prompt him by asking, *What about the embryos?*

Instead, she held her tongue and waited for him to find the words he appeared to be tossing around in his mind.

Finally, he said, "It's not something I have to do right away."

It *wasn't?*

"I'm not in any real hurry," he added.

The tightness in her chest eased, making it easier to breathe, to think, to speak.

"Your plan sounded pretty solid—and imminent—to me," she said.

"Actually, I'm thinking about postponing things for a while."

That was a good sign, wasn't it? Maybe he wasn't so gung ho on having his and Mary's babies, after all.

Not that Selena would have any objections to his using those embryos if his motive for doing so was right. She completely understood his wanting to have them because they were a part of him. It was only natural that he would. But if he planned to have them as a way to keep a part of Mary alive, then Selena couldn't get involved with him. It would be too risky.

However, it now sounded as if he wasn't so all-fired determined to hire a gestational carrier.

Did that mean his heart was finally on the mend?

And if so, had Selena been instrumental in the healing process?

Alex took her hand and gave it a gentle squeeze. "Would you feel better about going out with me if my plan to have those babies was further down the road?"

Yes, but she didn't want to admit it. Not when there was an even bigger question looming before them.

"Would *you* feel better?" she asked.

"Probably."

They stood there for a moment, so much hanging in the balance. More than he probably realized.

"Before you go," he said, "I have a question I'd like to ask you."

She braced herself for that heavy conversation she hadn't been ready for just moments ago, fearing an emotional gunshot to the heart.

"All right," she said. *Shoot.*

"There's a line dancing contest down at the Stagecoach Inn next Friday night. I think it would be a lot of fun to watch. Would you like to go with me?"

Was he asking her on a date? It certainly seemed that way. Moments ago, she would have turned him down flat. But now?

"Do you have to work?" he asked.

"On Friday? Yes, at the office. But I'm not on call, if that's what you mean." Still, she didn't come out and agree to go, even though she was sorely tempted.

When was the last time she'd kicked up her heels or did something just for the fun of it?

Not often enough.

"Have you ever been to a honky-tonk?" he asked.

She chuckled at the thought, releasing the last bit of tension that had built up in her chest. "I can't say that I have."

"Then you're in for a real treat."

She didn't know about that. She'd never been a big fan of country music, but by the crooked grin splashed across Alex's face, she got the feeling that she'd been missing out on a little known secret.

"I'll tell you what," she said. "I'll think about it."

"Fair enough."

They continued to stand there, as if waiting for something else to happen, something elusive. An opportunity Selena might never have again.

"You'd better get out of here," he said, taking a step back.

He must have read the surprise on her face because he smiled and added, "You're going to be late to that meeting, remember?"

"Oh. Yes. You're right. I can't forget that."

Still, she waited a beat before slipping behind the wheel and closing the driver's door. Then she started the engine, continuing the pretense that she had to rush off to a meeting she'd never scheduled.

And wondering just what the heck one wore to a honky-tonk.

Alex hadn't talked to Selena in more than forty-eight hours, not since they'd ridden horses up to Ol' Piney. But he hadn't seen any reason to. He knew she'd be at the wellness center on Tuesday night. They'd have plenty of time to talk afterward.

When she'd left his house Sunday afternoon, he'd gone out on a limb and mentioned the embryos, telling her he would postpone hiring a gestational carrier for a while. Because she'd agreed that the future was complicated, he'd begun to think that the whole baby plan might be holding her back.

And, apparently, it had been.

Of course, he hadn't changed his mind about having those children. He was determined to go forward with the plan. He owed it to Mary—and to himself.

But if he was interested in dating Selena—and he definitely was—they'd need to spend more time together to see if they were actually as suited as they seemed to be. If they were, and if things became serious enough to consider a long-term relationship, they could discuss the whole idea of his raising the babies or the two of them raising them together.

At that point, if Selena wasn't on board with his plan for the near future, then he'd know that they weren't meant for each other.

But why end their friendship—or whatever it was destined to become—before it even had a chance to get off the ground?

For that reason, as he drove to the wellness center Tuesday evening, he was determined to date Selena. After class, he would ask her out to dinner again, just as he'd done last time. He'd level with her about how that kiss had affected him—and what he'd like to do about it.

He'd already asked her to go to the line dancing contest at the Stagecoach Inn on Friday, although she hadn't agreed yet. But he'd do his best to talk her into it.

Once he arrived at the wellness center, he parked his truck, entered the building and made his way to the community classroom.

Just as he'd done both Tuesdays before, he took a seat in the front row and waited for Selena to arrive.

He'd had a devil of a time trying not to peer over his shoulder to look at the door each time it opened. But that didn't stop him from glancing at his wristwatch every now and then.

She was a few minutes late tonight.

When she finally made her way to the front, her high heels clicking on the linoleum, Alex sat up straight and offered her an it's-good-to-see-you smile, which she returned before placing her file upon the podium.

She wore a white lab coat over a black dress tonight, and she'd applied a fresh coat of lipstick. A classy lady, inside and out.

"Good evening," she said, glancing out at the others in the classroom. "I'm sorry I'm late. Let's get started."

As she began to speak about the difference be-tween surrogates and gestational carriers, her focus was clearly on her class and the lecture she'd prepared. But Alex was too caught up in the lovely instructor to process what she was saying.

The spark of attraction that struck hard each time she was with him darn near blazed right now, making it impossible to take note of anything other than how beautiful she was, how bright, how…

How weird was that? This was the one lecture he'd been waiting to hear. But he'd be damned if he could wrap his mind around any of it.

He'd missed her more than he'd expected to. And just being in the same room with her again had his pulse and his hormones doing all kinds of wacky things.

Still, he managed to pull a few sentences out of the air and made a mental note or two. As he'd expected, there were things he needed to watch out for in choos-ing a gestational carrier as well as other considerations he hadn't realized.

While Selena continued to talk about surrogacy, Alex studied the list of agencies she'd given the class, the handout she'd given him last week. He'd stuck it in his rear pocket, and they hadn't mentioned it since.

He'd never put much stock in Freudian theory, but he couldn't help wondering if they both wanted to avoid talking about his quest to have those babies.

Was that because he'd been right? That Selena wasn't interested in dating a man with kids?

Or was it merely his fear that his baby plan had her

dragging her feet about getting involved with him, when the kids had nothing at all to do with it?

Either way, he supposed it didn't matter. He'd give their relationship a chance to blossom, then he'd move ahead on his game plan. After all, what would it hurt to postpone things for a couple of months—six at the most?

When the class finally ended and everyone's questions had been answered or at least addressed, several women and one couple went up to the podium to speak to Selena privately. Most of them thanked the doctor for her time and expertise, but a few wanted to share their personal struggles.

Alex remained in his seat until everyone finally filed out of the classroom, then he walked up to the podium.

"How about dinner?" he asked. "I've got a hankering for tacos, and I have a feeling you haven't had a chance to eat yet."

"I had a late lunch, so I'm really not very hungry."

"Then have a salad or a cup of soup, something light. Please? I'd really like you to come with me tonight."

"Why?"

"Because we need to talk."

Selena reached for the file that held her notes and handouts. "About what?"

"All the things we should have discussed while we were at Ol' Piney."

Her gaze sought his, her eyes narrowing as if trying to read something in his words or his expression. But he couldn't blame her for that. He'd been keeping his thoughts and feelings to himself for most of his life. Or maybe all of it. He'd learned to clam up early on, when his father had clamped down on him at the dinner table, saying that children were to be seen and not heard. Even after he'd gone to live with his maternal uncle, a man who believed certain things—like feelings and other weaknesses a man might have—ought to be kept close to the vest, the lessons had continued.

Mary used to complain about that, although she'd gotten pretty good at getting him to speak up sometimes—and second guessing him when he didn't.

Selena tucked a strand of hair behind her ear. "I thought we *did* talk about…*things.*"

Not without her forcing the issue. And if truth be told, Alex had held back a lot. But marriage to Mary had kind of softened him a bit, and he'd learned to be more up front with a woman he loved.

Not that he loved Selena at this point, but who knew what could develop if they spent more time together?

"You were right to get angry with me," he said. "When I went to water the horses."

Her head cocked slightly to the side, her hair cascading down her shoulder.

"I really dropped the ball," he added. "That kiss was out of this world, and I should have told you so. At the time, discussing something as complex as a relationship seemed too soon and I just… Well, I guess you could say I balked."

"Why the change of heart?" she asked.

He shrugged, holding back the truth. Okay, so some

old habits were hard to break. But he wasn't ready to lose out on an opportunity to date Selena and see what became of it. Neither did he want to risk laying all that on the line and having her throw it back at him. So he offered her another reason on the list, which was just as honest but a bit lower in terms of importance. "I've enjoyed our time together."

Her once-guarded expression relaxed, and a hint of a smile tugged at her lips. "I've liked it, too."

"Good. Then let's go to Anita's tonight."

She pondered it for a beat before saying, "All right. You drive a hard bargain." Then she tossed a smile his way before taking her file of notes and placing it in her handbag.

Alex still planned to hire a gestational carrier, of course, but why scare Selena off with his family plan before they'd had a chance to decide if they were willing to be a couple?

Once he knew that she was in it for the long run, he'd add two newborn babies to the mix.

In the meantime, while they were dating, he would do a little more research on those agencies that were on the list she'd given him. He could also look over the information that Family Solutions was sending to him.

But Selena didn't need to know about any of that just yet.

Anita's was located in one of several two-story houses on Third Avenue, just three blocks from the quaint shops that lined both sides of Main Street.

At one time, the redbrick building had been the home of Edmond Calhoun, Brighton Valley's first mayor. Back in the 1990s, the Calhoun family had sold the property to Dale "Sully" Sullivan, who'd converted it to a bakery and sweet shop. But about ten years ago, the baker retired and moved out of state. So Sully put the house back on the market.

Shirley Salas and her husband purchased the building next and turned it into a restaurant. Because most of Shirley's recipes had been handed down to her from her husband's mother, she'd named the eatery Anita's, after her mother-in-law.

It hadn't taken long for word to travel, and Anita's soon became a favorite of the locals.

Not only was the setting homey, with its antique furnishings and colorful southwest artwork, but also the food was to die for. In fact, some of the dishes were almost as good as the meals Selena used to have when she visited her *abuelita,* who'd been, at least in Selena's opinion, the absolute best Mexican cook in the world.

Because Anita's was located just down the street from Selena's house, she and Alex decided to take both vehicles and meet outside the restaurant.

Finding a parking space wasn't always easy in this part of town, especially during the lunch or dinner hours, so Selena left her car in her own driveway and went inside the house, where she left her lab coat. She also took a few extra minutes to apply a fresh coat of lipstick and to run a brush through her hair. Then she walked several tree-lined blocks to meet Alex.

Just as she'd suspected, he had arrived first and was now waiting for her.

He stood near the steps that led to the entrance, a grin splashed across his gorgeous face. Even without boots and a hat, the man had a boatload of cowboy charm that Selena found amazing—and more than a little appealing.

"Have you eaten here before?" she asked as she joined him on the sidewalk.

"Every chance I get. How about you?"

"Not nearly as often as I'd like to."

"Then I'm glad I chose the right place." He placed his hand on her back and walked with her up the steps. After opening the door, he followed her inside the restaurant.

A silver-haired hostess wearing a turquoise peasant -style blouse and a black skirt greeted them with a friendly smile. "Good evening. Welcome to Anita's."

"Two for dinner," Alex told her.

The woman gathered up the menus, then stepped away from her station. "Please come this way."

They crossed the ceramic tile floor to the carpeted stairway. As the hostess led them up to the second floor, the lights overhead flickered off and on.

"Goodness," she said, slowing to a stop. "I'm not sure what's going on with that. It's happened a couple of times this evening."

When the flickering stopped, she continued to lead them to a room that had once been the Calhouns' library.

Selena scanned the wall-to-wall shelves laden with books, giving it a unique setting.

"It's been a slow night," the hostess said. "So you'll have the room almost to yourselves."

The only other diners in the room, an elderly couple seated near a cozy brick fireplace, were drinking coffee and having flan for dessert. So they'd probably be leaving soon.

Indicating a white-linen-draped table for two near a window that looked out on the street, the hostess asked, "How's this?"

"It's fine," Alex said, pulling out a chair for Selena. "Thank you."

They'd no more than settled into their seats when the busboy brought them water with lemon, a basket of warm chips and a bowl of salsa.

"Your waiter will be right with you," the young man said, before leaving them to study their menus.

Selena really hadn't needed to look over the offerings. She'd decided on a bowl of albondigas when Alex had mentioned it earlier this evening. The traditional Mexican meatball soup had always been a family favorite.

After the waiter, a heavyset man in his mid- to late-fifties, took their orders, they munched on chips and salsa while making small talk.

Alex asked her about college, about her decision to go to medical school.

"I wanted to be a doctor for as long as I can remember," Selena said. "So going to med school was a given."

In spite of her efforts to put Max Culver, her college sweetheart, out of her mind, Alex's question about school triggered the memory she'd tried hard to forget.

While in her second year of school, she'd actually considered marrying Max. In fact, she'd even thought about changing her major to something that wouldn't require as much education or as many student loans to secure a degree. But then Max had thrown a wrench into those plans, which ended up being a good thing, she supposed.

Once she'd licked her wounds and shaken off her disappointment, she'd focused on her studies, graduating with honors.

"How did you end up in Brighton Valley?" Alex asked.

"I did my residency at the medical center here, then went to work with Dr. Avery for a while. When I learned he was retiring, I took over his practice."

Before Alex could quiz her anymore, the waiter brought their food—the taco combination plate for him and a bowl of soup for her.

They'd only begun to eat when the lights flickered again.

"There must be a short in the wiring," Alex said as he scanned the room.

Selena glanced out the window, spotting the streetlight that shone steadily, suggesting the problem was limited to the restaurant. When she returned her gaze to Alex, the electricity went out.

"Well, thanks to the fire in the hearth," Selena added, "we're not completely in the dark."

"I guess we can consider this an unexpected adventure."

And a rather romantic one at that.

Yet before she could savor the aura and the handsome man sitting across from her, Selena's cell rang. If she weren't a doctor, she might have ignored it, but the tone told her it was the hospital calling.

"Excuse me, Alex." She reached into her purse and pulled out the phone. When the line connected, she answered, "Dr. Ramirez."

"Selena, it's Darren Chin. I just admitted Bella Hastings, one of your patients. Since you have a note in your chart to be notified if she went into labor, I thought I'd better give you a call."

Bella had miscarried three times in the past and had finally made it to the seventh month. Selena cared about all her patients, but Bella was special.

"Thanks, Darren. Tell her I'll be right there." Selena ended the call, then looked across the table at Alex. "I'm sorry. I need to go to the hospital."

"I didn't realize you were on call tonight."

"I'm not. It's just that… Well, I have a high-risk patient who's gone into premature labor. She and her husband have struggled with infertility for years, and she's gone through a lot of heartbreak. So I'd like to be there."

"I understand."

Before Selena could respond, the waiter approached their table holding a flashlight. "I'm sorry, folks. The electricity is out, and the kitchen has shut down for the night. So we have to close for safety purposes."

"No problem," Alex said. "If you'll get our bill, we'll be on our way."

"Actually, our cash register isn't operating, so your meals are on the house tonight."

Selena scooted her chair away from the table and stood, waiting for Alex to do the same. Then she grabbed her purse.

The waiter shone his light, leading the way to the stairs.

When they reached the door and stepped outside, the streetlight illuminated their steps as they made their way to the sidewalk.

"Does this happen to you very often?" Alex asked.

"What do you mean? Power outages, or hospital calls?"

"Both, I suppose. We've been to restaurants on three occasions, and you've had to help a woman in premature labor the first time and now you're rushing to the hospital to see about another. That's two out of three. And then, back at the ranch, there was Gus."

She found herself smiling at his assumption. "No, I'm afraid that's a little unusual. Why?"

"I just figured it might be par for the course when a man dates a doctor."

Is that what they were doing? *Dating?*

She supposed they were.

Her heart twisted at the thought of the risk she was taking by getting involved with a man who might never forget his late wife. But something told her there was a better question she ought to be asking herself.

Did she dare not to?

Chapter Eight

Outside Anita's, Alex stood with Selena under the golden glow of the streetlight, reluctant to say goodnight, yet knowing she needed to hurry.

"Thank you for dinner," she said.

He chuckled. "It was on the house, remember?"

She smiled. "Still, you invited me."

"Then you're welcome."

Alex placed his hand on Selena's shoulder. "Come on, I'll give you a ride."

"Thank you," Selena said. "I'll take you up on the offer."

Overhead, the evening sky was filled with bright, twinkling stars, and the autumn air was crisp. It would have been a nice night to walk Selena home, rather than drive her.

He would have been tempted to slip his hand in hers, to let her know how proud he was of her, how glad he was to be her...

To be her what? Her friend? That didn't quite cut it. But then again, "girlfriend" sounded juvenile.

Lover came to mind. And if he'd actually had the opportunity to walk her home, to wait for an invitation to come inside...

Instead, he opened the passenger door and waited for her to climb into his truck. Then he slid behind the wheel and backed out of the parking space.

"Where to?" he asked.

"Five blocks north, then take a right on Hawthorne."

When they reached the intersection she'd mentioned, he headed right on Hawthorne, a tree-lined street with homes that had been built in the late 1940s and early 1950s. The neighborhood appeared to be quiet, and the kind Norman Rockwell might have used as a model for some of his artwork.

"This is it." Selena pointed to a pale yellow house with brick trim and a dark green door. "It's not much, but it's where I call home."

Alex wasn't sure why she downplayed the place. It certainly looked appealing to him, with its manicured lawn and all the lush plants and flowers that lined the path to the stoop. Two ceramic pots of red geraniums flanked the front door, which sported a floral wreath.

He pulled along the curb and shut off the ignition. Before he could slide out of the driver's side, go around to her side and open the door for her, she let herself out.

"So what time will you pick me up Friday evening?" she asked as though it was all decided.

He couldn't stop a smile from stealing across his face. The last they'd left it, she was going to think about going with him to the Stagecoach Inn.

Apparently she'd decided to go. And he was grateful for that. It was nice to know they were both feeling a natural pull toward romance.

"The line-dancing competition starts at eight," he said. "Is seven o'clock too early for me to pick you up?"

"No, that's fine."

He waited a beat, then did what he'd been dying to do all evening. He kissed her good-night.

As he'd come to expect, her taste was just as unique as her scent, and so was the way she melded into his arms. A man could get used to kissing her senseless. And as much as Alex was tempted to kiss that soft spot behind her ear, to trail kisses along her throat, to let the hormones and pheromones take over as they moved on to the next step toward intimacy, he released her instead, knowing she had to go.

"Good night," he said. "Sleep tight."

"You, too."

He offered her a parting smile, then turned and headed back to his truck.

If he'd ever had any qualms about dating Selena, their arousing kisses had taken care of that. They'd also left him planning to give her a good-morning kiss in the very near future.

* * *

True to his word, Alex arrived at Selena's house a few minutes before seven on Friday night. When the doorbell rang, she'd just come out of the bedroom, where she'd been double checking her appearance. After all, she didn't wear snug-fitting jeans very often, so she couldn't help taking another gander in the full-length mirror to study the way the denim hugged her hips.

She looked all right, she supposed. But instead of seeing the familiar professional woman who usually peered back at her, her image reflected a small-town Texas gal who reminded her of the teenager she'd once been.

Of course, tonight she filled out her cotton T-shirt and jeans in a way she'd never been able to do back then.

Okay, enough of that. Shaking off any lingering insecurity, she hurried to answer the door, where she found Alex standing on the stoop.

He wore the cowboy garb she'd seen him in the first night she'd met him—boots, jeans and a Western shirt, as well as a heart-thumping grin that set her heart on edge.

As he scanned the length of her, the boyish glimmer in his eyes morphed into a full-blown, dazzling smile.

She ran her hands along her hips, dreading the way those old insecurities crept back after she'd done her best to shake them off just moments ago. But she'd never been to a honky-tonk before, so she hoped she'd chosen the right thing to wear.

"You look great," Alex said, as if he'd been reading

her mind or sensing her uncertainty. "Every cowboy in the place will be doing double takes at you all night long. I'm going to have to stick close to you so some other guy doesn't try to horn in on my position."

She almost told him that he didn't have a worry in the world, which was the truth. But she wasn't ready to make a revelation like that yet. So she tossed him a playful grin instead. "I doubt that'll be the case, but if so, you're the only cowboy I'm going home with."

Going home with? The moment the words rolled off her tongue, her cheeks warmed at the unintended sexual innuendo.

If Alex thought anything of it, he didn't say anything, thank goodness. So rather than dwell on the slip of the tongue or draw attention to it, she reached for her purse, which she'd left by the front door.

"You know," Alex said, as he stepped aside to let her out of the house, "I probably should have asked you if we could go earlier than this."

"Why is that?"

"Because the Stagecoach Inn is a popular place, especially with the TGIF crowd, and it's probably going to be tough to find a parking space."

"Then why don't you leave your car here? It isn't all that far. I don't mind walking. Besides, the weather's been especially nice today."

"All right. That sounds good to me."

After Selena locked the front door, they started down the sidewalk together.

It was still light out, but the setting sun had already

begun to paint the western horizon in amazing shades of pink, lavender and gray.

She wondered what the sky would look like hours from now, when their date was over. There would be a full moon, she suspected, and a scatter of bright stars. It would probably make a lovely ending to their date, a romantic sight on their way home.

Without conscious thought, her slip of the tongue came back to mind. *You're the only cowboy I'll be going home with.*

That was true. And the thought of inviting him into the house was far more appealing than it should be.

Or was there a good reason inviting him in—to the house or her bed—was so appealing?

Why fight something that was merely a natural progression to romance? After all, if their goodnight kisses were any indication of how good sex would be, making love was sure to be magical.

Maybe she ought to see how tonight went, then decide what to do.

When they reached the end of Hawthorne Lane, they turned on to Third Avenue. Other than the sound of their boots tapping on the sidewalk, they remained silent.

Finally, Selena asked, "Do you like country music?"

"I practically grew up on it," he said. "I like the beat, the words, the stories the lyrics tell. How about you?"

"I've never been a big fan. I've always preferred jazz or soft rock."

"You may change your mind after tonight."

Something told her tonight was going to change a lot of things.

Ten minutes later, they arrived at the Stagecoach Inn, which sat along the county road. Just as Alex had predicted, the parking lot was busting out at the seams.

"You were right," she said. "The place is really hopping. Is it always like this on a Friday night?"

"It's usually busy every weekend, but the line dancing competition is a special event."

As they crossed the graveled parking lot to the entrance, their boots crunched on the dirt.

Selena was looking forward to her first peek inside a real honky-tonk. She'd passed the Stagecoach Inn many times and had always been curious about the cowboy bar as well as its patrons. So once they entered, she found herself studying the interior, the scuffed and scarred hardwood floor, the antique red-and-chrome jukebox, the Old West-style bar that stretched the length of the building.

"Come on," Alex said. "I see a table. We'd better snag it before someone else does."

They made their way to the back of the room, not far from an orange neon sign pointing the way to the restrooms, and took a seat near a couple of cowboys who'd been drinking all afternoon, if the empty beer bottles on the table were a clue. They weren't dressed as nicely as Alex, but not many men stood out in a crowd like he did.

A couple of minutes after Alex and Selena had claimed their seat, a blonde, harried waitress stopped by and asked, "Can I get y'all a drink?"

Selena was just about to ask for a glass of red wine, when the waitress noticed Alex and recognition splashed across her face. "Well, I'll be darned. Look what the cat finally dragged in. It's been a long time, Alex."

"It sure has."

The bleached blonde studied him a couple of beats longer than usual. All the while, Alex seemed to be doing the same thing to her.

Had Selena been wrong when she'd assumed he hadn't gotten involved with another woman, that he hadn't had sex since his wife died?

Her stomach clenched at the thought, and she couldn't help wondering what kind of connection the two of them had.

"It's good to see you out and about," the waitress told him.

"Thanks, Trina. I figured it was time. How've you been?"

"All right." The waitress he knew by name turned to Selena, but instead of asking for her drink order, she studied her for a moment. Assessing her, it seemed.

Why was that? Jealousy? Or just run-of-the-mill curiosity?

"Selena," Alex said, "this is Trina Shepherd. She's an old friend."

Oh, yeah? How old? Where had they met?

The fact that having answers to her growing number of questions mattered more than she'd like it to was a little unsettling, but she shook it off and extended her hand for the customary greeting. "It's nice to meet you."

"Trina," Alex said, "This is Dr. Selena Ramirez. She's an obstetrician in town."

"Oh, really?" Trina tucked a stringy strand of hair behind her ear. "Are you the same Dr. Ramirez who took over Dr. Avery's practice?"

"Yes, I am."

The woman brightened, shedding a couple of unearned years from her face. "I've been meaning to make an appointment to see you. Dr. Avery was my obstetrician, and it seems I'll need one again."

She was pregnant?

The cocktail waitress sighed, then glanced at Alex and clicked her tongue. "I swear, my mother was right. I never learn from my mistakes."

Selena, who would love to have an unexpected pregnancy, couldn't help a momentary twinge of envy. But she shrugged it off as quickly as it came. It wouldn't do to dwell on her misfortune, especially when she had a practice full of expectant mothers.

"How far along are you?" Selena asked.

"Eight weeks and six days, to be exact." Trina blew out a sigh. "I won't need an ultrasound to figure that out."

Still, the sooner Trina saw a doctor, the better. She needed an exam as well as some prenatal vitamins. Pregnancy was going to take a lot out of her, and she already appeared to be tired, and maybe even undernourished.

"If you call in on Monday," Selena said, "ask for Maryanne, who sets my appointments. Tell her we met this weekend, and that I said I'd squeeze you in—even if it's during the lunch hour."

"Thanks. That's really nice of you. As soon as I get the kids off to school, I'll make that call." Trina glanced down at her notepad, then at Alex. "So what would y'all like to drink?"

Selena asked for a glass of merlot, and Alex ordered a Corona with lime.

"You got it." Trina scratched out their requests on the pad, then headed to the bar.

When she was out of hearing range, Alex said, "Thanks for offering to squeeze her in as a favor. Trina doesn't get many breaks."

It didn't seem like it. Selena leaned forward and lowered her voice. "Something tells me she's not happy about being pregnant."

"I'm sure she isn't. She already has her hands full raising two kids without any help from her ex-husband—financial or otherwise."

Apparently, she'd gotten involved with men who were neither supportive nor loyal. But then again, some women made the mistake of falling for a man who would never return the love she deserved.

Selena certainly had, so she was in no position to pass judgment. But that didn't quell her curiosity. "So where did you meet Trina?"

"She was a friend of Mary's."

At the mention of Alex's late wife's name, Selena's stomach clenched again. But he didn't seem to give it more than a passing thought, which she hoped was a good sign that he was moving on, that his love for his late wife would soon be a memory.

At a table next to theirs, a man who'd been drinking something amber-colored, like whiskey or scotch, threw back his head and laughed. Then he got to his feet, taking his glass with him.

"Tell Trina to bring us another round," he told his friend. "I'm going to make a pit stop, then I'll give Darla a call and ask her to come on down here and get us. We're going to need a ride home."

Still chuckling, the happy drunk started toward the bathroom. When he passed by Alex's chair, he swayed on his feet. In an effort to regain his balance, he flung out both arms. As he tried to prevent a tumble, the drink slipped out of his hands, splattering on Selena's shoulder before hitting the floor and shattering.

"Oh, damn," the drunk said to Selena. "I'm sorry, ma'am. I… Aw, hell. Would you look what I did?"

A bit annoyed, Selena studied her wet T-shirt, wondering if the brown liquid would leave a stain. "Maybe I'd better go to the ladies' room and wash this out." Then she got to her feet.

"I'm sorry," Alex said.

Selena gave a little shrug. "You didn't spill the drink on me."

No, he didn't, but he'd brought her to a honky-tonk, where this sort of thing could happen. And a beautiful, classy and professional woman like her might not appreciate close encounters with inebriated cowboys.

"I'm really sorry about spilling my drink," the sloppy

but remorseful drunk said to Alex. "I'd be happy to buy your lady a new shirt if that stain don't come out."

Alex might have made an issue about the spill if the guy had been a jerk about it. As it was, he shrugged. "Those things happen." He just wished it wouldn't have happened to Selena.

About that time, Trina arrived with a plastic tub and a damp rag.

The cowboy went down on one knee, prepared to help her clean up the mess on the floor.

"Daryl," Trina said to the drunk, "please get out of the way and let me clean up that spill and the broken glass before someone slips or gets cut."

"Sorry about that, Trina." The man got to his feet and took a step back. "I didn't mean to cause all this trouble."

"I know you didn't." Trina set the tub on the floor, then began picking up the biggest glass shards. "But the last thing I need is for a customer to get hurt. Bob's on his way with a mop to help me. You go on back to your friend."

When Daryl took off toward the restrooms, Alex said, "You shouldn't be doing that in your condition."

She glanced up. "Doing what?"

"Picking up broken glass and mopping spills."

Trina chuffed. "This is all in a day's work, whether I'm at home or here. Don't worry about me."

Alex did worry. Trina hadn't just been a friend of Mary's; she'd been his friend, too. After Mary's accident, he'd spent a couple of evenings at the Stagecoach Inn, trying to drown his grief and guilt. And Trina had made sure that he'd gotten home safely both times. She'd also reminded him that Mary wouldn't have wanted him to go off the deep end like that, and she'd been right.

When a man with a mop approached Trina, he asked, "What have we got here?"

"Just another day in cowboy paradise," Trina said, as she got to her feet. "I've already picked up the biggest pieces of glass."

"All righty. I'll take it from here."

"Thanks, Bob." Trina turned to Alex. "I'm sorry for the disturbance."

"No problem. Things happen."

"Yeah, they do." Trina glanced at the chair Selena had just vacated. "She's a pretty lady, and obviously smart and successful. Are you two dating?"

Mary and Trina had been friends as teenagers, so it felt a little weird to be out with another woman, even if it had been two years since Mary's death. But the question called for an answer, even if he wasn't quite sure he could say they were actually "dating."

"This is our first official date," Alex admitted. "But after tonight, she might realize she doesn't like my idea of a fun evening."

"I suppose you'll find out if she's a good sport or not when she returns from the restroom."

That was probably true.

"Either way," Trina added, "it's nice to know you're

finally getting out and living again. Mary wouldn't have wanted you to hole up at home."

Alex hadn't been in town all that much, but that didn't mean he'd been hiding out and avoiding people. He'd just found that hard work and staying busy had helped. And there was always plenty to do on a ranch.

"So how's it really going?" Alex asked her, trying to steer the conversation off him and Mary.

Trina shrugged. "Same old, same old."

He was sorry to hear that. Life hadn't been easy for her, and not all of her trouble had been of her own making.

She was only thirty-six, although she appeared to be a lot older. At one time, a lot of men would have found her pretty. But that was before she'd made a few bad choices.

And before life had kicked her while she'd been down.

Now she was pregnant again, which was too bad. The last Alex had heard, she'd finally gotten a divorce from an abusive husband she'd held on to for too damn long.

"It seems that I can't pick a nice guy if my life depended upon it," she said. "So I'm going to swear off romance once and for all. It's pretty clear that I'm not good at weeding out the jerks from the keepers."

Before Alex could respond, Selena returned, sporting a big wet spot that had soaked through one sleeve and the shoulder of her T-shirt.

But at least she wasn't frowning. Did that mean she actually was a good sport?

Somewhere in the midst of all the background noise and the hoots of laughter, the old red-and-chrome jukebox jumped to life, thanks to someone's desire to hear a little music before the band had set up for the evening's competition. Over the din, Alex heard Patsy Cline singing "Crazy," one of her biggest hits.

Call him crazy, but he was going to take a gamble on Selena being a good sport—and more. So he pushed back his chair and stood, then he reached out his hand to her. "Come on. I really like this song. Let's dance."

The suggestion seemed to take her aback for a moment, and she glanced at her wet T-shirt. He thought she was going to decline. Instead, she smiled and let him draw her to her feet.

Alex led Selena through the throng of Friday night revelers to a dance floor, where a few other couples had already gathered.

Then he opened his arms, and she slipped into his embrace. As they slowly moved to the music, he savored the floral scent of her shampoo, the silky strands of her hair.

It had been a long time since he'd enjoyed holding a woman close—and it had been forever since he'd held one quite like Selena. Without a conscious thought, he drew her close and placed his cheek against hers.

As Patsy sang about a love gone wrong, Alex couldn't help thinking about one that was going right. And he found himself lost in the music, completely under the spell of the woman in his arms.

It was magic, all right. Even with the other couples beside them.

He'd never really liked getting out on the dance floor and preferred to watch this sort of thing as a bystander. In fact, that's why the line dancing competition had interested him.

But that no longer seemed to be true, at least not when he held Selena. Not when he wanted to nuzzle her neck, to kiss her senseless, to take her to bed.

As they swayed to the music, it was easy to pretend that they were an actual couple and not just skating around a relationship.

And maybe they weren't skating. Maybe they both knew where they'd wind up this evening.

He certainly did.

Chapter Nine

Spending Friday evening at the Stagecoach Inn had been more fun than Selena had imagined, and she was glad that she'd gone.

The whole honky-tonk experience had been a blast, but more than that, being with Alex had made it a night to remember. And it wasn't over yet. Not while they were taking a slow, leisurely walk home under a scattering of bright stars and a nearly full moon.

"You were right," Selena said, as their arms brushed against each other. "I enjoyed the dance competition, but what I found even more interesting was watching all the people who'd come to hang out at the Stagecoach."

"The cowboy crowd can be pretty entertaining," he said.

"That's for sure." She'd also liked slow dancing with

Alex, his arms wrapped around her, his cheek pressed against hers, his woodsy cologne snaking around her senses, holding her captive.

"I'm glad you had a good time. When that cowboy spilled his drink on you, I thought you were history."

A smile teased her lips. "I couldn't get angry at a guy who fell all over himself trying to apologize and to clean up his mess. Besides, he was respectful. He was also responsible. When it happened, he'd been on his way to call his girlfriend to pick him up, rather than drive himself home."

"She was a pretty good sport about it," Alex said.

Selena had thought the same thing when she'd first seen the woman who'd come to take him home within ten minutes of his call. She'd crossed her arms and appeared to be scolding him, but there'd been affection in her eyes.

He'd called her his darlin' Darla, and in a way, their relationship had seemed…sweet. And loving.

Strangely enough, it was easy to be a bit envious of them and what they'd apparently found together. She wondered if Alex had noticed it, too.

"I could be wrong," Selena said, "but they seemed to have a good relationship."

"That's possible, but she might have given him hell when she got him home."

"I don't think so."

Alex didn't respond, and they continued to walk in silence, their steps echoing in the night.

They'd be home soon—in just a few short blocks.

Would he try to kiss her again? She certainly hoped he would. If he didn't, she might have to take the bull by the horns and be bolder than she'd ever been before, at least in a budding romance.

Their arms brushed again, and this time Alex reached for her hand, curling his fingers around hers, warming her from head to toe with a single touch.

Yes, he was going to kiss her goodnight. She was sure of it. But did she want him to stop at that?

As they turned down Hawthorne Lane toward her house, she imagined them a couple, with no concerns in the world. But she had plenty to worry about. What if she did the unthinkable? What if she fell head over heels in love with a man whose heart would always belong to another woman?

She knew firsthand how badly a situation like that would turn out. But the possibility of heartbreak in the future didn't seem to matter right now.

In spite of the need to protect herself from being hurt, she couldn't let Alex walk away tonight without giving him a chance to prove her wrong. So she lowered her guard and chose to ignore her apprehension.

By the time they reached her house, her heartbeat was soaring in anticipation. Just how far would they go tonight?

As far as he was willing, she decided.

He walked her to the front door, then waited for her to reach into her purse for her key.

"Would you like to come in?" she asked. "I can make some coffee or tea for us. I also have wine…."

"You decide. I'll have whatever you're having."

"Okay. Then I'll open a bottle of merlot."

"Good choice."

His words were compliant and polite, yet his tone was suggestive—and full of promise. Did he know what she was thinking? What she was hoping? Maybe even planning?

Oh, for Pete's sake. She wasn't even sure what she had in mind, just that she wasn't ready for the night to end.

"Do you want some help with the wine?" he asked.

"No, I've got it. I'll be back in a flash." She offered him a parting smile, then left him in the living room while she went in search of the bottle of merlot she'd been storing since she'd received it in a gift exchange during last year's hospital Christmas party.

As she reached the doorway, she had to force herself not to glance over her shoulder and take one more gander at the handsome cowboy she'd love to…love.

And maybe even seduce.

Alex stood in Selena's living room and watched her walk away. He'd planned to kiss her good-night on the stoop, but he'd been hoping for a lot more than that. So her invitation to come inside, to have a glass of wine, suggested that she'd been thinking the same thing.

As he waited for her to return, he scanned the cozy room, checking out the colorful artwork on the walls as well as the overstuffed green sofa and chairs. On a table near a built-in bookshelf, he spotted a Bose stereo.

Should he turn on some music? Would she think he was being presumptuous if he did?

Aw, what the heck. Why not? The anticipation in the silence was almost deafening. So he crossed the room to the stereo, which had a stack of CDs nearby.

It didn't take long to find something soft and mellow, something to set a romantic mood.

As the melody filled the room, he lowered the volume. Then he took a seat on the sofa, just as Selena entered carrying a tray with two glasses and an uncorked bottle of red wine.

"Service with a smile," he said.

"And a little background music. That's a nice touch." Her eyes, the color of rich Tennessee bourbon in the lamplight, brightened, kicking his pulse rate up a notch.

After she set the tray on the coffee table, she sat on the center cushion, just an arm's distance from him.

Yes, he decided, they were clearly on the same page.

He reached for the bottle of merlot and poured them each a half serving, then handed one of the goblets to her.

"Thank you."

"My pleasure."

He lifted his wine to her in a toast. As she clicked her glass against his, the crystal resonated crisp and clear.

"To...friendship," he said. "And whatever that might bring."

She smiled, giving him reason to believe that she'd heard the subtext behind his words.

As much as he'd like to take things slow and easy,

his feelings for Selena had gone beyond friendship. And he wanted to have a sexual relationship with her—perhaps even one that was lasting.

Of course, his future would one day include his babies, so there was still that hurdle to cross. But they had plenty of time to discuss kids, family and anything else that the coming months might bring their way.

As he savored a taste of the merlot, he pondered the decision he'd just made, the strength of his feelings for her, the possibilities that laced the pheromone-charged air. It had been a long time since he'd had to take the romantic lead, but it seemed natural to do so now.

In the background, a Michael Bublé CD played softly. Rather than risk an awkward attempt at conversation, Alex set his glass on the table in front of them and reached for her hand. "Dance with me, Selena."

Her intoxicating gaze locked on his, as she let him draw her to her feet.

He led her around the coffee table and to an empty space in the center of the room. When he opened his arms, she stepped into his embrace.

As they moved to the music, he held her close, their bodies pressed together. What he wouldn't give to have this night last forever, but the song ended long before he was ready to release her and return to the sofa for more small talk.

Instead, he wanted to kiss her senseless. And that's just what he set out to do.

While his arms remained around her, he drew back

long enough to see the unspoken emotion in her eyes, to watch her lips part, to hear her breath catch.

That was all he needed. He lowered his head and placed his mouth on hers. As their tongues met and mated, his blood pumped strong and steady. His hands slid along her back, stroking, caressing, exploring each womanly curve.

Finally, when they came up for air, he asked the question that had been burning inside him for days. "What are we going to do about this?"

"I'm not sure. I can tell you what I'd like to do." The glimmer in her eyes convinced him they had the same idea.

"I hope you don't plan to send me home," he said, his own eyes glimmering, no doubt.

"No, I don't want to do that. Not yet." She took his hand. This time she did the leading—to her bedroom.

He was glad he'd thought to bring a condom with him, even though he hadn't been sure if they'd have need of one.

If he hadn't been so caught up in the heat of the moment, in the desire to make love with her all night long, he might have told her they were in luck. But then again, maybe she was prepared, too.

Once in the bedroom, Selena made her way to the bed, then turned to face him.

Damn, she was beautiful. And tonight, she was all his.

He took her in his arms again and kissed her, long and deep. As he explored the curve of her back and the slope of her hips, a surge of desire shot through him, reminding him just how long it had been since he'd had sex. And if truth be told, it had been months before Mary's death.

She'd been so afraid of losing the babies that she hadn't wanted to make love once the implantation had taken place.

And he'd been okay with that. He'd understood the maternal hormones that had been at work. But right now, his male hormones had built to the bursting point.

If the kisses he'd shared with Selena meant anything at all, making love with her was going to be amazing— the kind of thing dreams were made of.

When the heated kiss demanded they move on to something more intimate, Alex drew his lips from hers, only to find Selena's gaze riveted on him. Rather than speak, she began to peel off her T-shirt, revealing a white lace bra, an expanse of skin...

He watched as she slid the fabric over her shoulders and removed her arms from the sleeves. She dropped her top to the floor, then unbuttoned her jeans and peeled them over her hips.

Before he knew it, she was standing before him wearing only her pretty, delicate undergarments.

"You're even more beautiful than I'd imagined, Selena."

Her cheeks flushed at the compliment, yet she still didn't respond. Instead, she reached for his shirt and tugged it out of the waistband of his jeans. Then she helped him remove it altogether.

When he stood before her, his chest bare, she skimmed her fingers over his skin. One of her nails sketched over his nipple. His gut clenched in reaction to the arousing touch, and he sucked in a breath.

Unable to hold off any longer, he lifted her in his arms and placed her on top of the bed. Then he reached into his front pocket and removed the condom he'd placed there earlier.

"You don't need that," she said.

He was glad to hear it, because he preferred not to use protection if he didn't need to.

"I'm not going to get pregnant," she added.

She seemed so certain that he assumed she was on the pill. Either way, she was a doctor; she obviously knew best.

"If you haven't been with anyone since…" She paused, her eyes searching his, clearly asking if he'd been with any other women after Mary had died.

He hadn't. No one had interested him until he'd met Selena. And because he and Mary had been tested for everything imaginable during the in vitro process…

Alex dropped the packet on to the floor. "We don't have anything else to worry about. We're safe all the way around."

After removing his jeans and boxers, he joined her on the bed and continued right where he'd left off, kissing, stroking, exploring…

When they were both overcome with need, he entered her. Her body responded to his, giving and taking, until they both reached a peak. As she cried out with her release, he let go with his at the same time, shuddering at the sheer pleasure of being one with the woman he...

Loved?

He didn't know about that, but it sure seemed like a possibility—and an amazing one at that. He could certainly get used to sleeping in Selena's bed, wrapped in her arms for the rest of his life.

As the last wave of their climax ebbed, he rolled to the side, taking Selena with him. He didn't have to ask if it had been good for her. He'd heard her passionate whispers, seen the pleasure in her eyes. Still, it had been more than sex to him. And he hoped it had been more than that to her, too.

As Selena lay stretched out on the bed, facing Alex, his arms around her, the sheets tangled, the sweet scent of their lovemaking fresh, she savored the amazing afterglow, unable to believe how good they'd been together.

In spite of her earlier apprehension, she couldn't help thinking that she'd finally met the one man she'd been waiting for all her life, a man who could give her everything she'd ever wanted—true love and a family, whether they adopted a baby or chose to use the embryos he'd created with Mary.

Of course, Selena would have to be convinced that she wasn't just a convenient replacement for the woman who'd died.

She had no way of knowing that, of course—unless she laid her heart on the line and allowed a relationship between them to develop. But she couldn't tell him what she was feeling.

Not yet.

She'd just experienced the night to end all nights, and while she longed to hear him say he felt the same way about her, she still feared that he wouldn't.

That he couldn't.

He pressed a kiss on her brow, then ran his hand along the curve of her hip and back up again. "It's only going to get better."

Her heart soared. So he wasn't content with just one night together either. He, too, knew that they'd found something special in each other's arms—a blood-stirring attraction, an awesome sexual connection and maybe even…love.

She placed her hand on his face, trailing her fingers on his cheek. "I can't imagine anything being better than that."

He smiled. "Neither can I."

She read sincerity in his expression, truth in his eyes. He either hadn't made any comparisons between her and his late wife, or if he had, Selena had come out on top.

"Do you have to go back to the ranch tonight?" she asked.

"Do you want me to?"

"No, I'd like you to stay for breakfast."

A grin slid across his handsome face. "I was hoping you'd say that."

He kissed her then, and she found herself wanting

to make love with him all over again. But it was more than a physical response to sexual stimulation going on. Her feelings were involved.

She nearly told him that she was falling in love with him, when in truth, she feared that she'd already toppled head over heels. And while she believed all the signs, sensing that he was falling for her, too, she just wasn't ready to admit it to him—or even to herself.

It's too bad they didn't have the entire weekend to explore their new feelings. She was on call tomorrow morning at eight, so in a few short hours she'd have to drive to the medical center and relieve the colleague who'd been covering for her.

But that was okay. Maybe after another bout of lovemaking tonight, she'd find the courage to tell Alex how she was feeling about him.

Somewhere around two o'clock, Selena had gotten out of bed and set the alarm so she wouldn't oversleep and run late for her shift. But she hadn't needed to do that.

Alex apparently had a built-in biological clock that woke him each day at the crack of dawn. So just like Sleeping Beauty of fairy-tale fame, Selena found herself awakened by a kiss.

"Good morning," Alex said as he sat on the side of the mattress.

Her lips slipped into a sated smile, even before her eyes opened.

"Coffee's ready," he added. "And breakfast will be on the table soon."

Selena glanced at the clock on the nightstand and realized the alarm was set to go off within the next ten minutes. "I didn't mean for you to do the cooking. I was going to do that."

"Maybe next time. I knew you had to work, and because I was the one who kept you up half the night, it only seemed fair to let you sleep as long as possible."

"That's amazing," she said, stretching and biting back a yawn.

He smiled, his eyes as bright as the morning sun. Then he brushed a kiss on her brow. "You probably ought to hold the compliments until after you've eaten."

"Okay, I'll do that." She returned his smile. "Do I have time to take a shower?"

"You bet."

Ten minutes later, Selena was dressed for the day and seated at the breakfast nook with Alex, tasting a fluffy batch of scrambled eggs and ham.

"This is wonderful," she said.

"You're just hungry."

"That's true. But my taste buds are still picky. Who taught you how to cook?"

"My housekeeper."

"Lydia?"

"No, the one we had when I was a kid living in Dallas." He took a sip of coffee.

"She taught you well," Selena said.

"That she did. She was a nice lady, and we were

pretty close. My mom and dad traveled on business more times than I could count, so I spent a lot of time with her."

How sad. If Selena was ever blessed with children, she'd covet the time she had with them. Of course, as a doctor with a busy practice, she might have to leave them with a sitter more than she'd like.

Maybe Alex's parents had had careers, too.

His father certainly had. Would he have spent more quality time with his son if he'd known his days were numbered?

The question gave her something to consider.

"It must have been tough to lose your dad when you were so young," she said.

"Yes, it was. But my uncle was good to me. He was strict, though, and didn't put up with any nonsense. But he wasn't as stern and demanding as my father had been." Alex dug his fork into the eggs and took a bite, as if the childhood memories no longer mattered.

Still, Selena hurt for the lonely little boy he'd once been. "Did your mom spend more time with you after you moved to the ranch?"

"Yes, but by that time, I preferred to spend time with my uncle and the ranch hands."

As she reached for her coffee cup, Alex glanced up from his plate and blessed her with an unaffected grin. "Actually, you would have liked my uncle."

"I wish I could have met him."

"He was one of a kind, a real cowboy with a dry wit." Alex sat back in his seat and slowly shook his head.

"One day, a stray dog showed up on the ranch, and I was determined to adopt him. My uncle agreed as long as I promised to keep him out of trouble. I figured it would be easy, but later that afternoon, one of the chickens got out of the coop, and the dog, Bear, took off after it. By the time I caught up with them, Bear had cornered the thing and chewed off its tail feathers.

"My uncle heard the commotion, came out of the barn and gave me heck."

"What did you do?"

"I stuck up for the dog, of course, saying it wasn't his fault. If the chicken had been in the coop where it belonged, it wouldn't have happened." Alex chuckled at the memory. "My uncle said, 'That chicken lives on the ranch, and that dog doesn't.' Then he shook his finger at me and said, 'Boy, if you don't get that mutt under control, he's going to be history.'"

"Did you get to keep the dog?"

"Yep, I sure did. Good ol' Bear was the proverbial boy's best friend."

"Whatever happened to the chicken?"

"That's the funny part, at least looking back on it. I told my uncle that I thought those tail feathers would probably grow back. And he said, 'They'd better. If I have to call the vet out here to see about that chicken, you're going to have to work a month of Sundays to pay the bill.'"

"Did he call the vet?"

Alex laughed. "He was just pulling my leg. If the dog had really hurt the bird, he wouldn't have bothered calling the vet. We would have had fried chicken that night for dinner."

She smiled, finding the story heartwarming. Still, she was sorry that Alex's early years had been sad and lonely, but it was nice to know that it had eventually worked out for him, that he'd found happiness on the ranch.

And with Mary.

Her heart twisted at the thought, but she did her best to shrug it off, to hold firm to the belief that he'd set memories of his late wife aside, that he was ready to embrace a new and maybe even better relationship with Selena.

"I hope I can be a loving and understanding father," he said.

"I'm sure you will be." She glanced at the clock on the stove, making sure she wasn't running late and re-alizing she'd have to go soon.

They finished breakfast in silence, and she wished that she had the guts to bring up the future, to ask when they'd see each other again.

Was he wondering the same thing? Was he consid-ering the logistics of having a lover who lived in town, while his ranch was at least fifteen miles away?

And what about the hours she kept, the nights she stayed at the hospital when one of her patients was in labor?

She supposed they'd find a way to make it work.

After finishing off the rest of her scrambled eggs, she lifted her cup and took a sip. Then she glanced across the table at Alex, whose brow was furrowed as though deep in thought.

"What's the matter?" she asked.

"Nothing, really. I was just thinking about something."

It appeared to be serious enough to force a smile from his face. "What's that?"

He set his cup down, then looked up and caught her gaze. "You know about my plans to hire a gestational carrier in the near future."

She nearly choked on the mouthful of coffee she'd just swallowed. The *near* future? What had happened to putting it on hold for a while?

"I was just wondering if—" he paused for a beat "maybe you'd be interested in the job."

Her?

"You'd be my first choice," he added with a smile.

His eyes glimmered, but she didn't find anything amusing about it. After all, she couldn't even carry her own child, let alone carry one for someone else.

And even if she could, did she want to be the means to an end? The uterus he needed to nurture Mary's babies until term?

The reality, the truth, the crushing disappointment balled up in her throat as her eyes welled.

"What's the matter?" he asked.

Her heart twisted, and she blinked back the tears. "I'm sorry, Alex. I can't do that."

He reached across the table and placed his hand on top of hers. "I'm the one who should be sorry, Selena.

I was way out of line to even bring something like that up—especially now. Please forget I said anything."

She'd never be able to forget that he still intended to have Mary's babies. Or that he thought Selena would agree to be a fill-in wife and mother.

But rather than let him know how badly she was hurt, she forced a wobbly smile. "It's already forgotten."

He paused a beat, watching her as if trying to read her expression, which she fought to keep hidden until she was ready to explain why his comment was so unsettling.

"Are you crying?" he asked.

"No," she lied. "I just have something in my eye." She blinked again, then used her fingers to rub away an imaginary lash or piece of lint.

After a quick glance at the clock on the oven, she got to her feet. "Oh, shoot. I can't believe this. I completely forgot I have an early appointment this morning. I need to go or I'll be late."

"Is there anything I can do to help you get out of here any sooner?" he asked.

"I wish there were." She left the kitchen in search of her purse—and a quiet place to wipe the telltale tears from her eyes.

Rather than slip into her bedroom, where the reminder of their lovemaking was too fresh, she hurried to the bathroom. There she tried to control her sadness until she could leave the house.

After she'd splashed cold water onto her face, she

went to find her purse in the living room, where Alex was waiting.

"I'll do the dishes and lock up your house," he said.

"Thanks. I'd appreciate that."

He followed her out to the car, where he bent to kiss her goodbye. She ought to object, to refuse his embrace, but she wasn't ready to explain why their all-too-brief affair was over. So she kissed him back as if nothing were wrong, when her whole world had imploded.

One of these days they'd have to talk about it, but not now. Not while the pain was so fresh, so intense. And not until she figured out a way to explain that it wasn't because of the babies. She didn't blame him one bit for wanting them. And if it weren't for his love of Mary, she might actually be thrilled to have the chance to mother them.

"Are you sure that comment I made about the...gestational carrier didn't upset you?"

"What comment?"

He seemed relieved. And so was she. This wasn't the time to talk about her objections, her pain, her disappointment.

She didn't trust her voice or her heart to provide more than a few words as an answer.

As she climbed behind the wheel, Alex said, "Drive carefully."

"I will." She shut the door and started the engine.

As she backed out of the driveway, he waved. Just as if nothing was wrong, she lifted her hand and fluttered her fingers.

Once on the road, she headed for the office, where she would face her patients and continue the charade, pretending that her heart wasn't breaking.

She wished she could say that the farther she drove away from Alex, the better she felt. But that wasn't the case. The ache in her chest intensified, and the tears she'd been holding back slid down her cheeks, one right after another.

Alex might have meant that kiss to be a way to end their night together, but it had actually been an end to whatever brief relationship they might have had.

Still, as sad as it was, as much as it hurt, Selena refused to be second place in Alex's life, to merely walk in the shadow of the woman he'd never forget.

Chapter Ten

Several days had passed since Alex and Selena had made love, and he had yet to talk to her.

Not that he hadn't tried. He'd called her on several occasions, only to leave a message on her answering machine or with her receptionist. He'd even given his name and number to her after-hours service.

At first, he figured she was either on call or at the hospital, delivering a baby. But it didn't take a membership in Mensa to come to the conclusion that she was avoiding him.

He'd be darned if he knew why. Time and again, he went over the conversation that had unfolded at her house that morning after they'd slept together, trying to figure out what went wrong and when.

That night they'd spent in her bed had been amazing.

They'd even cuddled together until dawn. Things really hadn't gone south until he'd tossed out that tongue-in-cheek comment about her being his gestational carrier.

He hadn't meant anything by it. He'd just thrown it out there as a way to gauge her thoughts and feelings about his baby plan. And to broach the possibility of her actually carrying his future children for him. She'd be invested in the pregnancy, in the children. But that had been too wild of an idea to ponder for more reasons than one.

Before they'd even slept together, he'd sensed she was apprehensive about his becoming a single father. And now it appeared that he'd been right.

She probably wanted to conceive a baby the old-fashioned way—her own flesh and blood, and not another woman's child.

If so, Alex could understand that. But he'd promised his dying wife he'd bring those embryos into the world one way or another. And that's exactly what he planned to do.

Had Selena really forgotten an early appointment at the office? Or had the mention of babies and a gestational carrier sent her running?

He supposed he'd never know for sure unless he got a chance to talk to her. He glanced at the telephone, wondering if he ought to give it one more try. Trouble was, he didn't want her to think he was that desperate to talk to her. After all, the phone line went both ways.

His first thought was to say, "The hell with it." If she

wasn't interested in him, if she didn't want a romantic relationship, then so be it.

But he was falling in love with her—if he hadn't done so already. And her not returning his calls was a complication he hadn't anticipated.

Again he reached for the receiver, tempted to pick it up one more time, only to cross his arms instead. He'd never had to chase after a woman in his life, and he'd be damned if he'd start doing it now.

He glanced at the clock on the mantel. It was getting late. The last time he'd called her at the house he'd left a voice mail. It seemed pointless to leave another one when she was clearly avoiding him. Maybe he ought to just turn in for the night. He could read for a while or catch the tail end of a movie.

As he got to his feet, the telephone rang and he nearly jumped. A glance at the caller ID told him the Brighton Valley Medical Center was on the line.

Okay, maybe Selena hadn't been at home today. Maybe she hadn't received all of his messages. Or if she had, she'd probably been extremely busy.

Or had she gotten sick or injured? He'd never even considered the possibility that she truly hadn't been able to call.

While tempted to snatch up the receiver in record time, he didn't want to appear too eager, too concerned, too ruffled. So he waited to pick up until the third ring.

"Hello."

"Alex?" The sound of his name rolling off her tongue set his heart on edge.

He wanted to blurt out, *What in the hell's going on? Why haven't you returned my calls? I know you're busy, but...* Instead, he maintained his composure and said, "Hey. How's it going?"

"All right. How are you?"

Angry. Confused. Hurt. But he kept that to himself and said, "Fine."

"It's been crazy busy around here."

Had it really?

"I can only imagine," he said.

"One of the other obstetricians in town had a heart attack Sunday morning, so I've been covering for him."

A sense of relief washed through him. Okay, so there was a good reason after all. Still, it was hard to believe that she hadn't been able to find two minutes to pick up a telephone or to reach for her cell.

"I'm sorry for not returning your call earlier," she added.

So she *had* gotten at least one of the messages he'd left. He steeled himself for an explanation, which he wasn't sure he'd buy, even if she offered it.

"There's really no excuse," she said.

He'd been right. She *had* been cooling her heels. The fact that she hadn't had the guts to be honest rubbed against the grain, and he couldn't help addressing the issue.

"I didn't expect a commitment, Selena. But after Friday night..." He paused, as the memory of their lovemaking unfurled in his mind. "Well, it seemed as though you shut me out before we had a chance to decide where we wanted to go from there, if anywhere."

Silence filled the line.

Finally she said, "You're right, Alex. I took the coward's way out. I care about you—a *lot*. And it's possible that whatever I'm feeling for you could turn into love. But I'm reluctant to get involved with anyone right now."

So she *was* giving him the brush-off. His first instinct was to pretend that it was no big deal, that it was actually a relief to him that they both felt the same way.

But disappointment wadded up in his throat, making it too difficult to speak at all, let alone to lie or feign indifference.

"Friday night was great," she added. "In fact, it was all I'd imagined it would be and more. But I have no business getting romantically involved with anyone right now. My focus is on my patients and my practice. So I wanted to… Well, I thought it was best that we lay that out on the table."

Oh, yeah? Then he was going to take a gamble and lay it *all* out there.

"It's not your practice that's bothering you, Selena. It's the fact that I plan to find someone to carry those embryos."

Again, her only response was dead silence, which spoke volumes.

"I admire your baby plan," she finally said. "I really do. I think it's awesome that you loved your wife so much, that you're so determined to have the children you were meant to have with her. But that's not something I want to be a part of."

There it was. The truth. As much as it hurt, he was glad she'd admitted it.

"Fair enough," he said. "If there's one thing I value in a relationship, it's honesty." *Even if it hurt like hell.* "So thank you for that."

Then he told her goodbye and ended the call. After all, there'd been nothing more to say.

Alex had not only promised Mary he'd find a way to have those babies, but he wanted them, too. He couldn't very well hold on to those frozen embryos forever. What was he supposed to do, offer them to someone else?

Or worse yet, destroy them?

His stomach knotted at the thought.

No, those kids—if they were destined to live—were his flesh and blood, his sons or daughters. And he'd do whatever he could to make sure they got the best possible chance to thrive—until birth and beyond.

And if that meant losing Selena for good, then so be it.

He just hadn't realized how badly it would hurt to let her go.

Alex waited three weeks for Selena to have a change of heart, for her to call or to stop by the ranch and say she'd changed her mind. But when that didn't happen, he followed through with his plan to hire a gestational carrier.

The agreement had been drawn up by Family Solutions. And the procedure was going to be costly—$80,000 plus medical expenses. But Alex had a good feeling about the agency as well as the woman he'd hired.

Kristy O'Malley was happily married with two healthy children of her own. Three years ago, she'd been a surrogate for an infertile couple in Wexler, so she knew what it was like to carry a child for someone else and to give it up.

All in all, Alex was pleased with his choice and with the entire process so far.

When he and Mary had gone through the in vitro process, it had been a nightmare—at least as far as Alex had been concerned.

First of all, before he and Mary had realized that she was unable to conceive without medical intervention, they'd gone through the whole clinical kit and caboodle, including morning temperatures and ovulation charts. Sex lost a bit of the magic when it had to be scheduled.

Then, after they'd found out their only option for conception was in a laboratory, the word *clinical* took on a whole new meaning. They'd removed nature from the equation, letting science take its place.

The months leading up to the first implantation had been enough to make a man think he might give up sex forever.

Well, not forever. But when push had come to shove, Alex would have preferred to have adopted a baby than to have gone through all that.

The counselor at Family Solutions had promised him

that the worst was over, as far as his part of it was concerned. And she'd been right.

He wasn't sure what Kristy had gone through, preparing for the implantation, but he'd only had to wait to hear that it had all gone according to plan.

And it had. According to David Samuels, the doctor at Family Solutions, as well as Kristy, the implantation had been a piece of cake. And when Dr. Samuels called with the good news—Kristy was pregnant with both babies—Alex was thrilled.

Okay, so he was a little insecure, too. But he planned to read books—a lot of them. And he'd ask questions, too. He'd… Well, he'd do whatever it took to be the best expectant father, as well as the best all-round daddy in the whole world.

He just wished Selena had been willing to be a part of it all. Not a day went by—not to mention a night— that he didn't think about her, dream about her. But she'd made her decision, and he had to abide by it.

For the first few weeks, Dr. Samuels had monitored the pregnancy. Once everything appeared to be on track, he asked if either Kristy or Alex had a preference of obstetricians or hospitals for the delivery.

While Alex probably should have left that decision to Kristy, he was the one who'd be footing the bill. So he'd said, "How about Selena Ramirez at the Brighton Valley Medical Center?"

"That's fine with me," Dr. Samuels said. "The decision is up to you—and to Kristy, I suppose."

After the call ended, Alex had run the idea past Kristy, and she was okay with it.

"No problem," she'd said. "I delivered at BVMC three years ago so I'm cool with that."

With that out of the way, Alex called Selena's office and spoke to the receptionist.

"I'm calling for Kristy O'Malley," he said. "I'd like to make an appointment for her to see Dr. Ramirez. She's six weeks pregnant with twins."

"How do you know she's expecting twins?" the receptionist asked.

"She just had an ultrasound at Family Solutions."

"Oh, I see."

When the woman asked about Kristy's insurance, Alex told her he was the father, and that he'd be paying cash—up front, if necessary. The babies, of course, would be covered under his health plan.

"We have an opening next Thursday at three," the receptionist said. "Will that be okay?"

It would have to be. He wanted Kristy to be under an obstetrician's care as soon as possible. But in this case, he was also eager to see Selena again, even if it was on a strictly professional basis.

Should he give Selena a heads-up before the appointment? Or should he just show up with Kristy in tow?

"You know," he said to the receptionist, "on second thought, I probably ought to make an appointment for a consultation with Dr. Ramirez first."

"All right. Why don't you take that three o'clock

on Thursday for the consultation. I can schedule Ms. O'Malley the following Monday at ten."

"That's great."

Alex just hoped it would be okay with Selena. But he couldn't think of another doctor he'd rather have deliver his babies.

On Thursday afternoon, a few minutes after three, Selena studied the chart her nurse had placed in the rack on the door, playing catch-up with the patient who was waiting in the exam room.

She'd met Trina Shepherd when she'd been at the Stagecoach Inn with Alex, and the pregnant waitress was now entering her seventh month. Both expectant mom and baby had been doing well.

The baby's father, who Trina hadn't thought she could rely upon, was back in the picture. At least, he had been at her last visit.

Selena gave a little knock before entering the exam room.

Trina, who'd been sitting on the table, broke into a happy grin. "Hi, Doctor."

The expectant mother was clearly a lot happier than she'd been on the night Selena had first met her at the Stagecoach Inn.

"How about that," Selena said, as she set the chart down on the counter. "You've certainly developed a healthy pregnant glow over the past few months."

Trina laughed. "Well, I'm not surprised." She held

up her left hand, where she sported a diamond on her finger. "Mark asked me to marry him, and I said yes."

"That's wonderful. I assume you're happy about it."

"I'm thrilled. And he's so good with the kids. I worried that he wouldn't be because he's never had any of his own. But I guess my old fears and baggage got in the way, and I didn't give him a chance to prove he was a completely different man from my two ex-husbands. I think I found a keeper this time."

Selena was glad to hear it. She didn't often get attached to patients, but there was something about Trina that tugged at her heart.

"So how about you?" Trina asked. "Are you and Alex still seeing each other?"

The question came out of the blue and struck fast and hard. Yet she found herself answering truthfully. "No, we're not."

"Too bad. He's a great guy." Trina gave a little shrug. "Just saying, that's all."

Selena wasn't about to discuss Alex or her decision with anyone, although Trina was right. Alex was one of the good guys, the white hats. And if there'd been reason to believe that Selena had a chance of being his one and only, she might still be seeing him.

After going over Trina's chart and determining that everything looked good, Selena measured the growth of her uterus and listened to the baby's heartbeat.

"Everything is coming along just fine," Selena said.

"Will I be having another ultrasound?"

"Actually, I'd planned to schedule one at your next appointment."

"That's great. Can I bring Mark in with me? He's never had a baby before, and… Well, I think he'd like seeing his son."

"Absolutely. I think it's great when fathers are involved with a pregnancy and delivery."

Moments later, after Selena told Trina to come back in three weeks, she moved down to exam room number two. As she picked up the chart on the door, she had no reason to believe that this afternoon would be any different from the rest.

And no idea that Alex Connor, who was already very involved in his children's pregnancy and delivery, was her three o'clock appointment.

After entering Selena's office and signing in with the receptionist, Alex took a seat in the busy waiting room.

It felt a little weird being the only man seated in an obstetrician's office. Well, that wasn't exactly true. He was the only man without a woman seated beside him.

But he'd better get used to being here. He planned to take an active role throughout Kristy's pregnancy as well as the delivery. So he shook off the uneasiness, reached for a copy of *Parents* magazine and listened for someone to call his name.

As he scanned the colorful pages aimed at the moms and dads with kids of various ages, he glossed over the articles, unable to focus on anything other than seeing Selena again.

She'd made it clear that her patients and her practice came first, above romance and a relationship. And he understood that. He just wondered how she'd feel when he asked her to be Kristy's doctor. He suspected that she'd be okay with it. Why wouldn't she?

But now that he was here, now that his heart rate had escalated and his blood was strumming through his veins in anticipation of seeing her again, he wondered if he'd made a mistake in calling her office for an appointment.

Could he keep emotions from getting in the way? He supposed he'd have to, or he'd need to choose another obstetrician, and he didn't want to do that. His babies deserved the best, and as far as Alex was concerned, Selena Ramirez was at the top of her field.

A door opened, and a middle-aged nurse wearing pink scrubs peered into the waiting room. "Kristy O'Malley?"

Apparently, the woman who'd made the appointments had gotten mixed up about who was coming when, but that was okay. He would just have to straighten it all out once he was behind closed doors. So he set down the magazine, stood and headed for the doorway.

"I'm Alex Connor," he told the nurse. "And I'm here for a consultation with Dr. Ramirez. Kristy's appointment is Monday at ten."

The nurse, with her graying hair pulled back in a twist, her brow furrowed and lips pursed into a frown, reminded Alex of one of his least favorite college professors, the one who'd given him a D minus in English

Composition. She glanced at the chart in her hand, obviously double checking the name on the paperwork.

"Kristy is the gestational carrier of my twins," Alex added, his voice lowered. "I'll be paying the medical bills, so I wanted a chance to speak to Dr. Ramirez before Kristy came in Monday."

"Oh, I see. Maryanne must have flip-flopped the names, but that's not a problem. We'll have everything squared away before Monday rolls around." The nurse looked up and smiled at Alex, no longer resembling the stern English prof. "Right this way."

Alex followed her past a scale and several exam rooms until they reached a small office with pale blue walls, a shelf of books and a view of the greenbelt below.

"Here we are," the nurse said. "Dr. Ramirez has her consults in her office, rather than in one of the exam rooms."

He was glad of that. He'd hate to have his first appointment with Selena be in small, sterile quarters, with him sitting on a paper-covered table and her on a stool.

The nurse indicated a cherrywood desk, with two chairs in front of it. "If you'll have a seat, I'll let Dr. Ramirez know you're here."

"Marge?" Someone called to the nurse. "You've got a phone call on line three."

"I'll be right there," Marge said to the woman who'd called her name. Then, as the woman approached, she handed over the file she held. "Maryanne, would you please give this to Dr. Ramirez and let her know the next appointment is a consult in her office?"

"Of course."

Marge turned back to Alex. "The doctor shouldn't be long. Why don't you make yourself comfortable?"

"Thanks."

As Marge left the room, Alex pulled out one of the chairs and took a seat. Then he scanned the small office, looking for photographs or personal items that would remind him of Selena.

Other than a bouquet of flowers near the window and an interesting watercolor behind her desk, it seemed liked a pretty generic office. That was a bit surprising because Selena was anything but generic.

He wondered what she would say when she heard he was here, rather than Kristy.

Either way, it really didn't matter now. He'd come too far to backpedal or to choose another obstetrician at this point—unless Selena wasn't interested in even becoming professionally involved with him.

But then again, why would she feel that way? She was a doctor. She'd learned to distance herself from her patients.

Hell, she'd even distanced herself from him, and he'd been her lover. Albeit for one night.

One amazing night.

His heart ached at the memory. Had he made a huge mistake in coming here?

Using Selena had seemed so logical. But how would it feel to be so close to her again, to have her treat him as a patient, instead of as the friend he'd thought he was, the lover he'd once been?

Right now, it wasn't looking good.

He glanced at his wristwatch, wondering how long he'd have to wait. But before he could ponder a guess, the door swung open, and Selena stepped inside, wearing a pink blouse and black slacks, with a white lab coat rounding out the ensemble.

At the sight of her in the flesh, his heart skipped a couple of beats, reminding him of how much he'd missed her.

Her lips parted and her eyes widened. Apparently, no one had told her about the mix-up, because she seemed to be doing her own assessment of him.

"Alex." His name rolled off her tongue softly, yet weighed down by emotion. "What are you doing here?"

Before he could find the words to tell her he'd gone ahead with his plan, she said, "I thought this appointment was with someone else."

"Kristy O'Malley?" he asked.

She glanced down at the name on the file, then nodded.

"I hired her to carry the embryos for me. And I wanted you to monitor the pregnancy and deliver the babies. That is, if you're willing to do that."

She seemed to struggle with an answer.

"I made this appointment to see you first, to ask if you'd mind." He studied Selena as if she held the whole world in her hands.

And in a way, she did.

* * *

Selena couldn't seem to make a move one way or another, into the office or back into the hall. Just seeing Alex again set her heart skidding through her chest. And not just because his visit had been a complete surprise.

"I'm sorry," she said. "I didn't have any idea you were coming in today. And… Well, it's good to see you."

Or was it?

Not a day went by that she didn't think about him. And not a night went by when he wasn't in her dreams.

"I'm sorry." Alex got to his feet and faced her, his hat in hand. "I didn't try to spring a surprise. They probably have me on the list for Monday at ten. But that's when Kristy is supposed to come in. I wanted to talk to you first."

Someone in the office had clearly screwed up, but she couldn't very well stand here, gawking at the handsome cowboy. So she pointed at the chair he'd been sitting in. "Why don't you take your seat? Let's start over."

As she made her way behind her desk, she still wasn't sure what to say. Certainly not the words that begged to be said, like, *I missed you. It's good to see you again. So very good.*

Instead, she cleared her throat and offered him a professional smile. "Congratulations, Alex. I know how badly you wanted those babies."

He smiled, as he waited for her to sit, then followed suit. "Thanks, Selena. I was very lucky. Both embryos implanted, so Kristy, the woman I hired, is expecting twins."

"I'm happy for you." And she was. Babies were a blessing, no matter how they were conceived. Besides, in spite of her decision to steer clear of him—romantically speaking—she wanted the best for him, for the family he was creating.

"So what do you say?" he asked. "Will you be Kristy's doctor? I wouldn't want her to use anyone else."

Selena was both touched and flattered. But could she get that involved with Alex?

How was she supposed to keep a professional air about her when she was attracted to the father-to-be? And not just attracted to him, they'd once been lovers. In fact, she'd fallen head over heels for him, which only made it worse.

So getting involved with him and his baby plan just wasn't right. Couldn't he understand that?

The way he was looking at her, leaning forward, gaze filled with hope, suggested he didn't have a clue what she was thinking or feeling.

"Under the circumstances," she began, "I'm not sure if it's a good idea."

"What circumstances?"

The fact that he could be the love of her life—if she knew that he felt that way for her. But that place in his heart would always belong to Mary.

Still, there were other circumstances that might make things difficult, awkward. So she leaned forward and lowered her voice. "Because we were lovers."

"How does that change the fact that you're one of the best doctors around, and that I want my kids to have the best?"

If truth be told?

She didn't have a clue.

Having those babies had been Alex's dream, and even though she'd been the one to end their relationship, it didn't mean that she didn't want him to be happy, that she didn't want the best for him.

So in spite of her reservations, she found herself saying, "Okay, Alex. I'll be Kristy's doctor."

He broke into a grin that sent her heart careening through her chest. "Thanks, Selena. I really appreciate this."

She knew he did. She'd just have to hope and pray that she hadn't made the biggest mistake of her life.

Chapter Eleven

When Monday rolled around, Selena didn't need to check the daily appointment list to know who'd be coming in this morning. Once she'd had the consultation with Alex and had agreed to be his gestational carrier's obstetrician, she'd been counting down the days until Kristy O'Malley's visit.

Sure, she was looking forward to meeting the woman. But more than that, she knew, without a doubt, that Alex would be attending that first appointment. The babies were too important to him. So there was no way he'd stay on the ranch and let nature take its course—at least, not after the babies had been successfully implanted.

By ten o'clock, Selena had already seen three patients and returned calls from two more.

So far, it was just a typical day at Brighton Valley OB-GYN.

But next up, in exam room three, Kristy O'Malley and Alex Connor waited for their first obstetrics appointment.

Selena paused at the closed door, going over the new chart, which held very little information yet, other than the vitals Marge had taken when she'd shown them to their room. However, it wasn't Kristy's blood pressure or heart rate she was concerned about, it was her own.

Right now, as she prepared to enter the room and see Alex again, as she readied herself to meet the woman who was pregnant with his twins, her pulse pounded in her ears. She would soon become fully engaged, fully committed to the pregnancy and to the health of the babies—Mary's babies.

But she couldn't stand here, bogged down by apprehension and a swarm of butterflies in her tummy. She was going to have to put on her big-girl/doctor panties and become the professional she knew she could be. So she rapped lightly on the door, then let herself into the small exam room.

Sure enough, a woman with strawberry-blond hair sat on the exam table. She appeared to be in her early to mid-thirties and of average height and weight. But it wasn't so much the new patient who'd commanded her attention. It was the handsome blond-haired cowboy who sat next to her, his hat resting under his chair.

Her heart rate spiked, and the blasted butterflies went

ballistic. How could he do that to her with a simple smile, a soul-stirring gaze?

Selena tore her attention from Alex, turned to Kristy and extended her hand. "I'm Dr. Ramirez."

"It's nice to meet you," the pregnant woman said. "Alex has been singing your praises."

Medically speaking, no doubt. Too bad he hadn't been singing more personal praises. But Selena couldn't allow herself to waste time on what-ifs.

"Alex mentioned that the implantation was done at Family Solutions," she said to Kristy. "How long ago was that?"

"It'll be seven weeks on Thursday," Kristy said. "I had a vaginal ultrasound a couple of weeks ago, and they saw both heartbeats."

After asking the standard questions, she quizzed Kristy about how she was feeling.

"Tired and a little nauseous, but nothing out of the ordinary."

Selena was glad to know Kristy had gone through several successful pregnancies already.

"Dr. Samuels said my due date is August twenty-eighth," Kristy added, "but he also said the babies would probably come early."

"He's right," Selena said. "Multiple births don't always go to term."

After giving Kristy a sample of prenatal vitamins to take and some healthy eating handouts, Selena added, "I'll order your medical records from Family Solutions as well as from the last obstetrician you used, if you don't mind."

"Not at all. My doctor was Bradley Leighton at Parkview OB-GYN in Wexler."

Selena made a note of it in the chart, then turned to Alex. "I'd like to give Kristy an internal exam on this first visit. So I'm going to ask you to step out of the room for a few minutes. When I'm done, I'll also do an ultrasound, which I'm sure you'd like to see."

"No problem." Alex got to his feet, then walked out of the room.

When the pelvic exam was over, Selena opened the door and asked Marge to wheel in the portable equipment. Then she called Alex back into the room.

Moments later, with Kristy lying on the table, her still-flat belly exposed and covered in gel, Selena ran the transducer probe over the uterus and watched the screen.

"There's the first baby," she said, as she located Twin A. "See the heartbeat?"

Alex eased closer. "That's amazing."

Yes, it was. And Selena never tired of looking at the miracle of new life. But even more than that, standing next to Alex, close enough to breathe in his scent, to see the wonder in his eyes, made her happy she'd agreed to be a part of this.

Her only regret was not being the woman on the table, studying the grainy, black-and-white images of the two tiny babies growing in her womb.

What Selena wouldn't do to be able to provide the

gift of life to herself as well as to Alex. As it was, she'd have to be content taking on a medical role.

Returning to the work at hand, she moved on to Twin B, whose heartbeat was strong and steady. "Here's the second one."

She waited for Alex to study the screen, then removed the transducer probe. After wiping the bulk of the gel from Kristy's lower belly with a tissue, she took a step back from the table, distancing herself and doing her best to remember her place.

Alex, who'd been standing by the pregnant woman's side, reached out and placed his hand on Kristy's shoulder. "Thanks for giving me the opportunity to be a father."

A twinge of envy reared its head, snaking around Selena's heart until it ached. But she had to face the facts.

Even the hired gestational carrier, a mother of two children herself, was able to provide Alex with something Selena would never be able to give him.

Alex nearly danced his way out of Selena's office that morning. He'd already seen the proof of Kristy's pregnancy during the first ultrasound at Family Solutions, although he'd pretty much had to take Dr. Samuels's word for it. But this morning he'd actually seen the two hearts beating.

Medical science was amazing, and Alex had been moved beyond measure. As he'd studied that screen, he'd tried to wrap his mind around the fact that he was going to be a father—to twins.

He had no idea whether they'd be boys or girls or one of each, but it really didn't matter. What did matter was that he was going to have a family again, that there'd be a reason to celebrate holidays.

After Kristy made her next doctor's appointment, Alex walked her to the parking lot, where they'd each left their cars. He wasn't quite sure what to say to her, other than to thank her one more time, which wasn't necessary.

"Do you have time for a cup of coffee?" he asked.

"No, I have a parent-teacher conference at the kids' school. So I'll have to take a rain check."

While she got into her sedan, he climbed into his pickup. But instead of heading home, he would spend the day in town. So he drove to Babies and More in nearby Wexler. There he ordered another crib and dresser, just like the set he already had at home. The set Mary had chosen and had planned to use for their daughter, if mother and child had lived.

For a moment, he ached for what could have been. Yet he knew Mary would have given her blessing for him to move on. Why else would she have made him promise to give the embryos life? She would want them to live that life to the fullest—to play Little League, to have a puppy, to join the Girl Scouts and take piano lessons.

Once Alex paid for his purchase and scheduled the delivery, he ran some other errands, including a stop at the feed store, where he placed an order for grain. While there, he called Shane Hollister, the Brighton Valley sheriff, and asked if he had time for lunch.

"As long as we can make it after one o'clock," Shane said, "lunch sounds good to me."

Waiting an hour or so wasn't a problem for a man dragging his feet about leaving town. So Alex agreed, then met Shane at Caroline's Diner a few minutes after one.

It was nice to catch up with the Brighton Valley sheriff, who'd had a baby girl a year ago last December.

"How are Jillian and little Mary Rose doing?" Alex asked as he picked up a French fry and dipped it into the dab of ketchup he'd squeezed onto his plate.

"They're doing great. It seems that Mary Rose was taking a few wobbly steps one day, then running the next. She sure keeps her mom and me on our toes."

Kids certainly grew up fast. Alex remembered when Mary Rose was just a newborn. The Hollisters had thrown a party at their new house just last December, when the baby had been only a few weeks old.

"I have some news of my own," Alex told his friend.

Shane reached for his glass of iced tea. "What's that?"

"Remember my plan to use those embryos?"

"You went through with it?" Shane set down his glass without taking a drink. "You hired a surrogate?"

Alex didn't see any point in explaining the difference between a gestational carrier and a surrogate to Shane. So he merely nodded and said, "The implantation was a success. If all goes well, I'll be the father of twins next summer."

"That's amazing."

Yeah, it was pretty miraculous. Even though he'd promised Mary he would do his best to see those embryos born, he hadn't been sure of the chances. And now, almost three years after Mary's death…

It was a shame she'd never have the chance to hold them, to mother them. But he'd have to be both mom and dad to them.

"Did you ever see an ultrasound of Mary Rose?" Alex asked Shane.

"Yes, I did. And it was awesome. I mean, I knew she was in there, but to actually see her hands and feet, her fingers and toes…" Shane slowly shook his head, a goofy grin splayed across his face. "It was priceless."

"Yeah, well, there wasn't much for me to see today— other than two tiny hearts beating. But I'm looking forward to watching them grow."

"Congratulations, Alex. I know how much this means to you."

"Thanks." It would have meant even more to have Selena's support, to have her understand why he had to do what he did, but Shane didn't need to know any of that.

The two friends went back to eating, and when they'd finished, Shane tried to grab the bill.

"Oh, no, you don't," Alex said. "It's my turn to pay. You got it last time."

After settling up at the front register, Shane and Alex walked out to the curb on Main Street.

"Are you heading back to the ranch?" Shane asked.

"No, I'm going to find things to do in town until late this afternoon."

"Why's that?"

"There's someone I want to see, and she doesn't get off work until then." He didn't see any point in telling Shane who the "she" was. How did he explain having a crush on the doctor who would be delivering his twins?

No, there were some things a man didn't discuss even with the best of his friends.

Two hours later, after Alex had hung out in Brighton Valley for about as long as he cared to, he headed back to Selena's office, where he told the receptionist that he wanted to speak to the doctor after her last appointment of the day. Then he took a seat in the waiting room.

This time, when he picked up the *Parents* magazine, he actually found a couple of interesting articles to read.

Apparently, there were plenty of books and periodicals that held a wealth of knowledge for a man wanting to learn about parenting and fatherhood.

Too bad there weren't any easy answers to be had for convincing a woman to give love a chance.

After Selena's last appointment of the day, she took a seat at her cherrywood desk and returned a couple of telephone calls from patients who'd left messages with the nurse.

She'd just hung up the phone when Marge poked her

head through the open doorway. "Dr. Ramirez, there's a man in the waiting room asking to talk to you."

"Who is he?" Selena asked.

"The guy who came in earlier today with the new patient, Kristy O'Malley."

Alex? Her heart stalled in her chest. Why would he come back to talk to her? Did he have a question he'd forgotten to ask?

"What should I tell him?" Marge asked.

"That I'll be right with him."

Marge nodded, then turned away, heading for the waiting room.

Selena could have followed right behind. Instead, she opened the bottom desk drawer, where she kept her purse. Then she reached for her makeup bag and pulled out a tube of lipstick and mirror.

As crazy as it was, as emotionally risky, she checked her hair, powdered her nose and reapplied a coat of Matador Red to her lips.

Then she made her way to the waiting room to greet Alex as if it was all in a day's work.

When she walked through the doorway, he stood and greeted her with a heart-thumping grin.

Would it always be like this? Would she struggle with attraction whenever he was near?

Should she have refused to be Kristy's doctor?

"Do you have time for a cup of coffee?" he asked, moseying toward her with a cowboy swagger. "Or maybe dinner?"

Yes. No.

"I need to talk to you," he added.

Did he? Why?

His gaze wrapped around hers, holding her captive, drawing her into his world, to his life. And against her better judgment, she found herself waffling and saying, "There's a coffee bar and newsstand down the street."

Minutes later, she'd grabbed her purse from her office and was crossing the parking lot with him, on their way to The Grind.

"So what did you want to talk about?" she asked.

He paused a beat, then said, "Us."

Her breath caught. He still considered them a couple? When they hadn't dated in months? When she'd told him that she needed to focus on her practice, on her patients?

"I'm not sure I understand," she said.

"I shouldn't have to explain, Selena. What we had together was special. And I'm not buying the fact that your career comes first. I think you're reluctant to date me because of the babies. And I suppose I can't blame you for that."

He thought that she considered his having kids a detriment, and that wasn't true. The fact that Alex had a child or two wouldn't be a problem. But she knew how happy he was to be having Mary's children. And the fact that he was anticipating the birth of the twins was a little...

Bittersweet, she supposed. And a constant reminder of the woman he'd loved, the woman he'd lost. And a reminder of what Selena could never give him.

Her steps slowed, and she turned to face him, her hand gripping the shoulder strap on her purse as if it could tether her to solid ground. "I care about you, Alex. More than I'd like to admit. But…"

God, she couldn't do it. She hated to admit that it wasn't just Mary she couldn't compete with. She couldn't even compete with his gestational carrier.

"But what?" he asked.

"I'm not ready to take on a ready-made family," she lied. "At least, not at this point in my life."

His gaze searched her face as if he might be able to uncover a lie, as if he knew she wasn't telling the entire truth. But she couldn't reveal more than that.

She refused to be second best or to play the fool again. And dating Alex, helping him parent another woman's children, would put her in that very position.

Everything she'd ever pinned her heart on—the old boyfriend from college, the dream of being a mother one day—had been stolen from her by fate or life or whatever. And being with Alex would only make things worse by subjecting her to more pain, more heartache, more rejection.

"Do you know what I mean?" she asked, realizing he didn't and hoping he'd accept her decision without forcing the issue.

"Sure," he said, his steps slowing to a stop. "I understand."

They stood like that for a moment, at a stalemate, a line drawn in the sand. Then he nodded in the direction of The Grind. "Maybe it's best if we pass on the coffee."

He was right.

There wasn't anything else to say. Not when they had no hope of a future together.

Nearly four months had passed since Selena had stood on the sidewalk near the coffee shop and told Alex one last time that she didn't want a relationship with him, yet not a day went by that he didn't remember their parting, the humbling moment when he'd went to her one last time, hoping for her to reconsider.

That evening was as clear now as if it had only been yesterday. He'd studied her for a beat before responding, hoping that she'd have a change of heart, that she'd hear the finality of her words and offer some hope that time would prove differently.

But she hadn't.

She might care about him, but certainly not enough to consider getting emotionally involved with a single father.

To say that he was disappointed was an understatement. But he'd accepted her decision. And her loss.

It seemed to be par for the course. Over his lifetime, he'd lost everyone he'd ever loved. And yes, he'd come to realize that he really did love Selena. Letting her go wouldn't have hurt him so badly if he hadn't. So even though her decision had been painful, it had been for the best.

As dusk had settled over them that winter evening outside her office, he could have sworn he'd seen her eyes glisten while she'd told him goodbye. And he'd briefly wondered if she might have been feeling something akin to remorse or maybe even a change of heart.

But she'd stood in silence, strong and resolute. So he'd turned and walked away.

At that point, he probably should have looked for another obstetrician for Kristy, but he wanted only the best for his children—and he still considered Selena to be the top in her field.

So from that day on, he'd stayed on the ranch and let Kristy attend her routine appointments without him. And because she always called him afterward, updating him, he was okay with that. And quite frankly, it was easier to not have to face Selena every three weeks.

He had no idea how he'd handle the actual delivery, though. It was important for him to be at the birth, although he wasn't entirely sure why, just that it was.

Still, even though four months had passed since he'd last seen Selena, he hadn't forgotten her, hadn't stopped wishing things had been different, that their feelings had been mutual.

He tried to tell himself that he'd done the right thing, that he'd fulfilled his promise to Mary. And in that respect, he had.

It was too bad Selena hadn't understood why the babies meant so much to him, why he had to go through with his plan in spite of knowing that his decision to move forward had squelched any future he might have had with her.

Sometimes, he'd find himself angry about the unfairness of it all—and angry at Selena for being so...

What? Stubborn? Selfish?

Hell, he couldn't blame her for wanting to raise her own children and not someone else's.

Besides, he couldn't very well stew about things like disappointment and anger when his babies—a little boy and girl—were doing so well.

For a moment, he remembered the day he'd seen them both on the ultrasound screen and learned their sex. He'd almost passed on attending that appointment until he'd learned that Selena was going to be delivering a baby, and that one of her associates would be running the scan.

Hell, if he couldn't even face her, how was he supposed to convince her to give him another chance?

No, he would abide by Selena's wishes, no matter how tough it was. And the best way for him to do that had been to focus on his growing son and daughter—and on Kristy's uneventful pregnancy.

Now, as he waited for his ranch foreman to return from the barn, Alex watched the sun rise on another beautiful April morning. He breathed in the fresh Texas air. As he surveyed the ranch that had once belonged to his uncle and would one day belong to his children, he watched a new colt frolicking in the corral with its mother. A smile stretched across his face. It was impossible not to count his many blessings on a day like this.

Life was good.

But before he could utter a small prayer of thanksgiving, Lydia walked out of the mudroom and called him to the phone.

"Can you take a message?" he asked. "I need to talk to Jake about the plans for the day. Who is it?"

"It's Kristy," Lydia called out. "And she said it's an emergency. She's already called Dr. Ramirez, who's going to meet her at the Brighton Valley Medical Center."

Oh, God. No. It was still too early for her to go into labor. The babies stood little chance, if any, of surviving outside the womb.

"What do I tell her?" the housekeeper asked.

Alex was already running to his truck, reliving the day he'd gotten the call from the Brighton Valley sheriff's office, telling him about Mary's accident.

"Tell her to call an ambulance," he said. "I'm leaving now. I'll meet her at the hospital."

He prayed he'd make it in time.

And that Selena would be able to help.

Chapter Twelve

Selena had just stepped out of the shower when her after-hours answering service called, relaying the message that Kristy O'Malley was headed for the hospital in an ambulance.

She gripped the receiver, her knuckles aching, while listening to what few details Kristy had given before hanging up and calling the paramedics. Apparently, she'd been having contractions off and on all evening. She hadn't thought too much about it until they started coming at regular intervals early this morning.

Fortunately, Selena had talked to her about being a high-risk pregnancy because of the twins. And she'd told her not to ignore any unusual aches or pains. In cases like this, it was always better to be safe than sorry.

In cases like this...

Selena's thoughts turned to Alex. Did he know yet? Would he be coming to the hospital?

Of course he would. Those babies meant the world to him, even though he hadn't come to any of Kristy's appointments since the very first one.

As Selena threw on some clothes, she pondered his reasons for staying away. Kristy had implied that he was busy on the ranch, as well as mentioning his involvement in training the horses for the new hippotherapy program at the wellness center. And Selena hadn't questioned that.

Still, a part of her wondered if Alex had been avoiding her for another reason. After all, she hadn't seen him since the day he'd asked her to reconsider dating him—and she'd told him no.

But she couldn't worry about that now. She had to get to the hospital to check on Kristy and the twins. At twenty-six weeks gestation, the babies stood a chance of making it. But on top of the health issues they'd face at birth, they would also be at higher risk for lasting disabilities.

Selena grabbed her keys and her purse, then headed for the door. After locking up the house, she climbed behind the wheel of her car, determined to get to the Brighton Valley Medical Center as quickly and safely as she could. She would do whatever she could to ensure those babies stayed in the womb as long as possible—for Alex's sake.

And maybe for her own sake as well. She'd been afraid to tell him how she'd felt about him, afraid to risk heartbreak. So she'd held back on the truth and had run like a scared rabbit.

For a moment, she indulged herself, imagining that Alex's feelings for her had been stronger than she'd thought they were. That she'd made a mistake by not trusting him to move on from Mary to her. But she shook off the starry-eyed musing, focusing on more important things to worry about now.

By the time she reached the hospital and found a space reserved for physicians, she hurried to the maternity floor and made her way to the nurses' desk, where Sylvia Ramos sat. "Has Kristy O'Malley arrived yet? She should have come by ambulance."

"We put her in labor room 235," Sylvia said. "Gretchen has her hooked up to a fetal monitor."

"Thanks."

Moments later, Selena entered Kristy's room and found her stretched out on the bed, wearing a standard hospital gown.

"What's going on?" Selena asked, as she made her way to her patient.

"I'm not sure. I'd been having some minor contractions last night. I thought they were probably Braxton-Hicks or false labor of some kind, but some of the pains were pretty sharp. And this morning, they were coming at regular intervals. You told me not to take any chances with that kind of thing, so I decided I'd better come in."

"I'm glad you did."

Because Kristy had given birth before, she knew

what to expect during labor. So Selena took her worries and concerns seriously.

"Excuse me, Dr. Ramirez."

Selena looked up to see Sylvia Ramos standing in the door way. "Yes?"

"The father of the babies just arrived."

Alex. Selena's heart thumped, and her pulse rate soared just knowing he was here.

"What should I tell him?" Sylvia asked.

"Tell him to go to the waiting room. I'll come and talk to him as soon as I've examined Kristy."

Selena had known that she would have to face Alex again someday. And the next time around, she'd planned to be more honest and up front with him than she'd been in the past.

She just wished their next meeting wouldn't have been during a crisis.

Alex had begun to wonder if Selena would ever come into the waiting room and let him know what was going on.

He probably ought to take a seat because all but two of them were empty. But for some reason, he found himself pacing the floor like the proverbial expectant father.

Yet instead of moving because he was a bundle of restless nerves, he was doing it out of fear.

What was going on behind those closed doors? The nurse he'd talked to at the desk had said Kristy was being examined. Was she in any kind of danger?

He certainly hoped not. And as badly as he wanted

the twins, he didn't want to see Kristy's health jeopardized in any way.

Finally, at a quarter to nine, he heard footsteps—a pair of high heels?—clicking in the hall. He turned toward the door, just as Selena walked in wearing a white blouse and black slacks. She looked just as pretty as ever, although she appeared to be a little windblown today, as if she'd hurried to dress.

Of course she probably had. Kristy would have notified her doctor before she'd called him.

Alex strode to the middle of the room, meeting Selena halfway. "How is she?"

"She's doing okay for now. She was having some preterm labor, but she really hadn't started to dilate yet. So I gave her some medication to stave off the contractions, and it seems to be working."

"Oh, thank God." He raked his hand through his hair, then asked, "What caused it?"

"It's hard to say at this point. But the babies seem to be doing fine."

He was glad to hear that, but he was also worried about Kristy. Her husband traveled a lot on business and was gone from home on most weekdays. So who was watching her kids and getting them off to school this morning?

And what if she had to stay in the hospital for an extended period of time?

He was paying her to carry the babies for him—and with twins there'd been a bonus. Yet even though she was being compensated for the inconveniences of the

pregnancy, he hadn't meant for her to have to spend
weeks or months in the hospital.

Selena placed a hand on Alex's arm, providing a
soothing balm without saying a word. The heat of her
touch sent him hurtling back in time to the days when
they'd first become friends, to the night they'd been
lovers.

He covered her hand with his, sealing her warmth,
possessing her touch for as long as he could.

"I know how worried you must be," she finally said.
"But for the time being, the babies aren't in any danger."

He continued to cover her hand, craving so much
more than that. "Thanks for the reassurance, Selena.
At times like this, I'm glad you're devoted to your job
and your patients."

"At times like this?" She smiled. "You mean there
was a time when you weren't?"

Yeah, as a matter of fact there was. Whenever he
thought about her and their time together, he resented
her dedication to her career, her practice. But how selfish had that been, especially now, when he needed her
dedication and skill more than anyone did?

Yet he was tired of pretending that her rejection
hadn't hurt like hell. Tired of rolling over.

The babies were a way for him to start a new life.
Not that he wanted to give up his ranch and all he'd built
there, but it wasn't enough. He needed a home, a family. And he wanted Selena to be a part of it.

For that reason, he'd do whatever it took to make sure
that happened, even if it meant taking the chance that

Selena would shoot him down once again. So, with his heart still raw with emotion from the fear his children were in danger, he let down his defenses.

"To be honest?" he said. "I'd hoped you'd be willing to become a part of a family. *My* family."

"I…" Selena stiffened and drew back. "We talked about this, Alex. I have a medical practice. And you have a ranch. We live in different worlds."

He knew that. And he appreciated her desire to maintain a career. As far as he was concerned, she could have it all if she wanted to. And he'd support her in any way he could.

Yet as he stood here, baring his soul, she'd retreated into a stiff cloak of professionalism.

She'd been so warm, so loving, so willing that night they'd spent together. She'd been more of a woman than a doctor.

And the fact that she was being so cool, so distant now, set off something inside of him. Something battered and bruised. And he didn't care who was listening or how vulnerable it made him sound.

"Selena, I love you. I didn't plan for it to happen, it just did. And I want us to be together for life—partners and lovers. If you'd be willing to be a mother to the twins, I'd be more than willing, more than happy to have another baby or two with you."

Selena's lips parted and her breath caught. "It's more complicated than that."

Yes, he supposed it was. So he released her hand and

took a step back. "Never mind. There's no need beating a dead horse."

She seemed to chew on that for a moment, then glanced at her watch and let out a sigh. "I really need to get to the office, but that'll have to wait. We need to talk."

Before he could respond, she took him by the arm and led him out of the waiting room.

Alex wasn't sure where she was taking him—or what there was left to say—but he would hear her out.

Selena's heart raced as she led Alex down the hall and into one of the private conference rooms on the maternity floor. But it was time to lay it all on the table— her apprehension, her fear.

As difficult as it would be to lay her heart on the line, to tell him why she couldn't date him, she had to come clean. She'd never given him a reason, which didn't seem fair. Especially now that he'd told her he loved her. And she feared it wasn't enough.

Once they were inside and had some privacy, she turned to face him. "I haven't been completely honest with you."

His head cocked slightly, but he didn't press her. Instead, he gave her the time to find the words that had to be said.

"I love babies, Alex. That's one reason I chose obstetrics as my medical specialty. And there's nothing I'd like more than to become a family with you, to mother your twins and to give you other babies someday. But I...can't."

"Why not?"

It was such an easy question to ask, but so difficult to answer. Especially when she'd been holding tight to her fears for so long.

"I love you, Alex. More than I care to admit."

"So what's the problem?"

She bit her bottom lip, holding back one last time. But Alex had forced the issue. And her fear of losing the babies he so desperately wanted far outweighed her fear of having her heart broken.

"I can't have children, Alex. I might be able to help bring them into the world for others, but that's as far as it goes for me. I can't get pregnant. And I can never give birth myself."

He reached for her hand and gave it a warm, gentle squeeze. "That doesn't matter to me. If we want more children, we can adopt."

"But there's more," she said.

"I'm listening."

She took a fortifying breath, then threw down the gauntlet that had become too hot to handle. "I'm not willing to be second place in your life."

Confusion splashed across his face. "I don't under-stand."

She slowly shook her head. "No, not the babies. They'd need to come first while they're so tiny and de-pendent. I'm talking about Mary."

The confusion in his expression deepened. "What about her?"

Selena took a deep breath, then slowly let it out. "You loved her deeply. And I'm afraid…" Again she paused before going on. "I'm afraid that I'd always be your second-choice wife."

He seemed to toss that around for a moment, facing the truth.

"As a side note," she added, "I hope to find a man like you someday."

His grip on her hand tightened, sending her senses as well as her hopes reeling. "You already have me now, Selena."

Was he kidding? She wanted to believe that, but… "I have you by default. And I need to know that you'd be able to love me as much as you loved Mary."

He reached for her chin, tilting her face and locking his gaze on hers. "You're right. I loved Mary. She was a wonderful woman, a good wife. But that doesn't mean I don't love you every bit or more than I loved her. You're different from her, and I love you in a unique and special way."

She wanted to believe him. Did she dare?

"If a mother has two children," he said, "don't you think she can love them both but in different ways? Her love for one has nothing to do with her love for another."

When he said it like that…

"Give me a chance to prove it to you, Selena."

There was nothing she'd like more.

She glanced at her watch one last time, then back to

Alex. "I need to go to the office. But don't worry, I'll be monitoring Kristy from there. I'll give you a call later this afternoon to let you know how things are going. And if they continue to go well, maybe we can set a time and place to meet and talk about this further."

"I'll wait for your call," he said. "And you're right. This conversation isn't over. In fact, I think it's just begun."

She nodded, then dashed out the door.

Did she dare hope that things might actually work out between them? That she might have the family she'd always dreamed of having—and with the man she loved more than anything or anyone else in the world?

By the end of the day, Selena was feeling pretty confident that the medication to stop Kristy's contractions had worked. So she called Alex with the good news as well as an update on the woman's family situation.

"Kristy's mother took some vacation time at work," Selena told him. "And she's going to stay with the kids while Kristy's in the hospital—and for the two weeks of bed rest I'm going to order."

"If this goes longer than that," Alex said, "if there are any other unexpected complications, I'll send Lydia, my housekeeper, over to help out."

"That's thoughtful," Selena said.

"Yeah, well, Kristy didn't plan for this to happen."

"Maybe not, but complications do arise. Family Solutions explains that to their surrogates and gestational carriers. It's one reason the process is so costly."

"Yeah, well…" He paused, as if struggling with his thoughts. "I'm still sorry that she's going through this."

So was Selena. And she was glad to know Alex had such a thoughtful side. After all, he really wanted those babies. Another man with the same dream, the same obsession, might have been too focused on his own concerns, his own worries.

"Do you have any questions for me?" Selena asked, hoping she'd been able to ease his mind already.

"Just one. You mentioned that we ought to talk. And because things seem to be going well, I wondered if you'd like to have dinner with me this evening."

Throughout the day, Selena had thought about the talk they'd had in the conference room, about hope that had sparked after his profession of love. And she was looking forward to discussing the future, to see where their love might lead.

"Sure," she said. "Where do you want to go?"

"How about Anita's?"

She loved Mexican food because she'd been raised on it. And she was glad he liked it, too.

"Another craving for tacos?" she asked.

"I suppose so. But I also feel badly about getting a free dinner there last time."

"The power went out. Remember?"

"I certainly do. So I'd like to patronize the place more."

Alex wasn't just a nice guy, but he was generous, too. Again she thought of how lucky Mary had been to meet him first.

But Selena felt pretty darn lucky, too.

"Okay," she said. "Anita's it is. I'll meet you there."

Twenty minutes later, Selena had run a brush through her hair and applied a coat of lipstick. Just as she'd done the last time they'd gone to Anita's for dinner, she parked her car at home and walked to the restaurant.

And as she suspected, Alex was standing on the curb, waiting for her. He tossed her a dazzling smile that spun her heart three-sixty.

No, make that one-eighty, because they were both headed in a new direction now.

At least, it certainly seemed that way.

He took her hand, and they walked up the steps together. Then he held open the door for her and followed her inside.

The same silver-haired hostess wearing a red peasant-style blouse and a pair of white slacks greeted them with a friendly smile. She reached for the menus. "Good evening. Two for dinner?"

Alex nodded. "Yes."

"Right this way." The hostess led them across the ceramic tile floor to the carpeted stairway. "You'll be in the library again this evening. But you should feel better knowing our electricity hasn't given us any problems since that night you were here."

"That's good," Alex said.

When they'd been seated and the busboy had given them water and a basket of chips and salsa, Alex said, "First of all, I want to thank you for all you did for

Kristy and the babies today. It was a comfort knowing you were in charge."

"You're welcome. Just so you know, it would have broken my heart to see you lose the babies after all you've done to get them here."

He gave a shrug. "It was something I had to do. When I make a promise, I keep it."

"You know," Selena said, "Mary was a very lucky woman." And for once, there wasn't any resentment or envy behind the words.

"I was the lucky one," Alex said. "She put up with all my faults."

Quite frankly, Selena hadn't seen many of them.

After a quiet dinner, Alex paid the bill. Then they walked outside. The clouds darkened the sky, hiding the stars. Yet the evening seemed brighter, more promising than ever before.

"Let me drive you home," Alex said.

"But it's only a couple of blocks from here."

"I know, but I was hoping you'd invite me inside. And I don't see any reason to leave my truck parked here."

"Neither do I," she said with a smile.

She couldn't imagine not wanting to extend their evening together, not inviting him into the house—and into her bedroom. Not making love to him, now that their life together held such promise.

After Alex pulled into the driveway and parked, they walked to the front door. She used her key, then led him into the living room.

She'd no more than turned on the lamp when Alex took her in his arms and pulled her close. She'd missed holding him, touching him, and she lay her head against his.

"Thank you for giving me a chance to prove how much I love you," he said.

"And thanks for hanging in there with me while I was running scared."

"You were worth it." Then he kissed her, slowly, thoroughly, as if they had all the time in the world.

And, as she'd just begun to realize, they really did.

When the kiss ended, Selena remained in his embrace, her heart soaring at the thought of what lay before them. Not just another incredible night of lovemaking, which she knew was just a few heartbeats away. But the birth of the babies, the creation of a family.

"I love you, Alex. And I'm looking forward to whatever the future brings."

He drew her close. "I love you, too."

Selena pressed a light kiss on his lips. "And I want you to know that I'll do my very best to mother the twins and to make Mary proud."

"Let's leave Mary out of this," Alex said. "From this day forward, it's all about you and me and the babies. Agreed?"

She nodded. "All right. It's a deal."

Then he kissed her one more time, sealing the agreement with a heart-strumming, soul-stirring kiss.

Selena had it all—a wonderful career, a man who loved her and the family she'd always dreamed of. She didn't think the future could look any brighter.

Epilogue

Selena couldn't believe all the changes that had taken place in the course of a single year.

Last May, she'd married Alex Connor in a small but romantic wedding ceremony at the Brighton Valley Community Church in front of their closest friends. Then, two months ago, she'd delivered her own newborns—a five-pound nine-ounce son and a six-pound one-ounce daughter—while the happy father, the love of her life, looked on.

It had been a real stroke of luck when Dr. Nathan Blankenship moved to town and joined Selena's medical group. His arrival had allowed her to take eight weeks off while he covered for her.

When it was time to return to work, she would cut back on her hours. Even then, it would be tough to leave the twins, but she knew that Lydia would love and care for them as if they were her very own.

So for the time being, Selena enjoyed the time to rock her babies and marvel in their sweet smiles and the joy they'd brought to her life.

Could any mother love her children more?

"Honey?" Alex called from the mudroom. "Is lunch ready yet?"

She lifted her finger to her lips. "Shh! I just managed to get Jonathon to sleep. He's been fussy all morning."

It was important for Jonathon to nap, just as his sister Caitlyn was doing, because Selena had plans to surprise her husband with some alone time.

Alex entered the kitchen, where Selena sat at the table with little Jonathon wrapped in a blue-and-yellow receiving blanket. He peered at their son, who snoozed in Selena's arms, and smiled.

"But to answer your question," Selena said, her voice lowered to a whisper, "Yes, lunch is ready. But you'll have to wait a while."

"Why? What's up?"

She got to her feet. "Is your horse saddled?"

"Yes, why?"

"Because I'd like you to saddle Sugar Foot for me, too. Just give me a minute. I'll put the baby in his crib and then let Lydia know I'm leaving."

"Where are we going?"

"I thought it would be fun to take a picnic lunch up to Ol' Piney. I also thought I'd bring a blanket along, just in case you had an urge to…nap."

A slow grin stretched across her husband's handsome face. "I'll have those horses ready to go before you can snap your pretty fingers."

He brushed a kiss on her lips. "And it's probably only fair to tell you that while I'd love to stretch out on a blanket with you, I'm not planning to do any napping."

"Neither am I." She winked, then got up from the chair, careful not to jostle the baby in her arms.

"I love being married to a woman full of surprises."

"You're a fun man to surprise, especially when you're not planning to nap."

Then she tossed him a grin before setting off on a romantic outing, which was becoming a marital habit she had no intention of breaking.

* * * * *

COMING NEXT MONTH from Harlequin®
Special Edition®
AVAILABLE SEPTEMBER 18, 2012

#2215 THE MAVERICK'S READY-MADE FAMILY
Montana Mavericks: Back in the Saddle
Brenda Harlen
Soon-to-be single mom Antonia Wright isn't looking for romance, single dad Clayton Traub only wants to make a new start with his infant son, and neither one is prepared for the attraction that sizzles between them....

#2216 A HOME FOR NOBODY'S PRINCESS
Royal Babies
Leanne Banks
What happens when a Texas nanny learns she is the biological daughter of a prince? Her rancher boss steps in to help protect her from the paparazzi, but who can protect her from her attraction to him?

#2217 CORNER-OFFICE COURTSHIP
The Camdens of Colorado
Victoria Pade
There's only one thing out of Cade Camden's reach—Nati Morrison, whose family was long ago wronged by his.

#2218 TEXAS MAGIC
Celebrations, Inc.
Nancy Robards Thompson
Caroline Coopersmith simply wanted to make it through the weekend of her bridezilla younger sister's wedding. She never intended on falling in love with best man Drew Montgomery.

#2219 DADDY IN THE MAKING
St. Valentine, Texas
Crystal Green
He'd lost most of his memories, and he was back in town to recover them. But when he met the woman who haunted his dreams, what he recovered was himself.

#2220 THE SOLDIER'S BABY BARGAIN
Home to Harbor Town
Beth Kery
Ryan fell for Faith without ever setting eyes on her. Their first night together exploded in unexpected passion. Now, he must prove not only that the baby she carries is his, but that they belong together.

You can find more information on upcoming Harlequin® titles, free excerpts and more at www.HarlequinInsideRomance.com.

HSECNM0912

SPECIAL EDITION

Life, Love and Family

Sometimes love strikes in the most unexpected circumstances...

Soon-to-be single mom Antonia Wright isn't looking
for romance, especially from a cowboy. But when
rancher and single father Clayton Traub rents a room
at Antonia's boardinghouse, Wright's Way, she isn't
prepared for the attraction that instantly sizzles between
them or the pain she sees in his big brown eyes.
Can Clay and Antonia trust their hearts and build the
family they've always dreamed of?

Don't miss

THE MAVERICK'S
READY-MADE FAMILY

by Brenda Harlen

Available this October from Harlequin® Special Edition®

*What happens when a Texas nanny learns she is
the biological daughter of a prince? Her rancher boss
steps in to help protect her from the paparazzi, but who
can protect her from her attraction to him?*

Read on for an excerpt of
A HOME FOR NOBODY'S PRINCESS
by USA TODAY *bestselling author Leanne Banks.*

Available October 2012

"This is out of control." Benjamin sighed. "Well, damn.
I guess I'm gonna have to be your fiancé."

Coco's jaw dropped. "What?"

"It won't be real," he said quickly, as much for himself
as for her. After the debacle of his relationship with Brooke,
the idea of an engagement nearly gave him hives. "It's just
for the sake of appearances until the insanity dies down.
This way it won't look like you're all alone and ready to have
someone take advantage of you. If someone approaches
you, then they'll have to deal with me, too."

She frowned. "I'm stronger than I seem," she said.

"I know you're strong. After what you went through for
your mom and helping Emma to settle down, I know you're
strong. But it's gotta be damn tiring to feel like you've
always got to be on guard."

Coco sighed and her shoulders slumped. "You're right
about that." She met his gaze with a wince. "Are you sure
you don't mind doing this?"

"It's just for a little while," he said. "You mentioned that
a fiancé would fix things a few minutes ago. I had to run it
through my brain. It seems like the right thing to do."

She gave a slow nod and bit her lip. "Hmm. But it would cut into your dating time."

Benjamin laughed. "That's not a big focus at the moment."

"It would be a huge relief for me," she admitted. "If you're sure you don't mind. And we'll break it off the second you feel inconvenienced."

"No problem," he said. "I'll spread the word. Should be all over the county by lunchtime. No one can know the truth. That's the only way this will work."

Coco took a deep breath and closed her eyes as if preparing to take a jump into deep water. "Okay" she said, and opened her eyes. "Let's do it."

Will Coco be able to carry out the charade?

Find out in Leanne Banks's new novel—
A HOME FOR NOBODY'S PRINCESS.

Available October 2012 from Harlequin® Special Edition®